NOCTURNES

T. R. STINGLEY

D0921005

FriesenPress

Suite 300 - 990 Fort St

Victoria, BC, Canada, V8V 3K2

www.friesenpress.com

Copyright © 2015 by T. R. Stingley

First Edition — 2015

All rights reserved.

No part of this publication may be reproduced in any form, or by any means, electronic or mechanical, including photocopying, recording, or any information browsing, storage, or retrieval system, without permission in writing from FriesenPress.

Aside from the fact that this might well be a recalling of a past life with my wife, all characters and circumstances as they might relate to anyone living or dead, or the living-dead, is purely coincidental. Also, no animals were harmed in the making of this novel. Nor were they tested on in any way. And thank you, sincerely, for reading my story.

ISBN

978-1-4602-7245-9 (Hardcover)

978-1-4602-7246-6 (Paperback)

978-1-4602-7247-3 (eBook)

1. Fiction, Mystery & Detective

Distributed to the trade by The Ingram Book Company

A writer depends, as much as any human can depend on anything, on a circle of friends and family who tirelessly remind him/her of their talent. I would be remiss not to mention my late mother, Sue Lewis, who sparked my love for literature at an early age. And my old friend Matt Hogan, who was with me all those years ago when I bought my first typewriter. And within that small circle, there is, it seems to me, one in particular who refuses to accept anything less than the fulfillment of the dream. That "one in particular" in this case is my wife, Tami. She has been my muse, my confidante, and the tireless advocate for whatever gifts the universe has lent me. This book is as much hers as it has ever been mine.

PRELUDE

He could feel it building. That all-too-familiar yearning was waxing anew. Soon, very soon, he would have to kill again. It was not a thing he took lightly. Most days, he would gladly trade places with nearly anyone. Anyone but a stage four cancer patient, or an AIDS sufferer… or the homelessly insane. He could only feel pity for those people. And that is why he would choose them over everyone else.

CHAPTER ONE
(SUMMER, 1996)

From the end of a long line of searching souls, the old man took a step and paused. Up ahead, over the bowed heads and shoulders of the faithful, he could see the tall, distinguished figure of Father Evan Connor. Step, and pause. Closer to salvation? One foot forward, and pause. Finally, he stood, hands clasped, before the priest. Father Connor looked into the old man's eyes, took two hosts and dipped them into the crimson wine. "The body and blood of Christ."

Amen. Isaac received the sacrament on his tongue and crossed himself with a trembling hand. Returning to the pew, he knelt and began the same prayer that he had whispered for more than forty years. This was the only hope that was left to him. And he would continue to cling to it unto death.

—— * ——

"Scat! Scat cat!"

The orange and black tabby scurried around to the street-side of the rambling brownstone that Isaac called home, followed in hot pursuit by the elderly man himself. Isaac was brandishing his infamous "cat broom," Bane of Felines, Scourge of the Cat-Kingdom, Widow Maker, Destructor. He closed in on the tabby as its paws scrambled for purchase on the leaf-littered walkway. Isaac emitted a low meowling that rose in pitch and volume as the broom rose over his head, readying for the swat that would send the cat sprawling across the uncut lawn.

Suddenly, a big, gray tomcat darted from beneath the front steps, circled Isaac's feet, and bolted after the tabby. Isaac swung the broom like a scythe, hoping for the rare double-spank, but only managed to disturb several elm leaves and a fur ball.

"The dried carcass of a previous victim, no doubt," Isaac grinned.

The cats gained the far corner of the house and turned in unison to see if he had given up. Isaac paused, then started a soft, casual whistle as he walked nonchalantly in their general direction, sweeping a few leaves from the sidewalk as he went. The cats allowed him to move within a broom's-length, then sprang quickly towards him. At his feet they split up and shot past him in a blur of snarling color. Isaac swung the broom wildly, making several noises intended to convey a religious conviction to the martial arts. The cats were not impressed. They scaled the wrought iron fence near the street and turned once more in a victorious smirk before sauntering up the avenue.

Isaac sat down on the steps, chuckling at their clever tactics. His weekly exercise accomplished, he leaned back against the cool cement, feeling considerably younger than his years. And if there was anything to be gathered from the faces of the two elderly women who had paused to witness his broom-wielding antics, he didn't act it either.

His neighbors considered him eccentric...a little off. He had lived alone in that house for more than twenty years, and was rarely seen except in the company of fleeing felines. He received few visitors and paid no calls.

He was rumored to be engaged in any manner of perversions, from serial killer to union sympathizer. Most folks in the neighborhood wondered how much longer it would be before they hauled the old man off in some anonymous van to some anonymous home, to eventually wither into an anonymous grave.

But Isaac had no intention of withering anytime soon. While he had formerly retired several years earlier, he remained a respected freelance writer for a handful of travel magazines. And while his life did not include an abundance of intimate friends, he was still a healthy, active, and intellectually-inquisitive man.

His cat-carnival was a source of fuel for the local gossip. He knew this. But he enjoyed the company of the cats. And they came from blocks around to participate in the games. The cats were certainly more tolerant than the faces watching him from behind narrowly-parted curtains. They depended upon his longevity, instead of anticipating his vacancy.

—— * ——

The late afternoon shadows hung like tapestries upon the otherwise barren walls as Isaac wandered restlessly among the quiet rooms. He had been packing for the past three days. Actually, he had been procrastinating for the past three days. He walked into the bedroom and gazed mournfully down into the suitcase. Two pair of socks and an undershirt accused him.

He was booked on the 15:10 to Atlanta, which meant that he had less than two hours to get to the airport. But his heart just wasn't in this assignment. The travel and timetable involved seemed rather overwhelming, even for a veteran of his stature. He was to cover eleven four- and five-star hotels in eleven different southern cities. Everything from wine lists to room service, all to be accomplished in less than a month. Just the thought of it all was enough to send him retreating to his wing chair with a tumbler of brandy and a good book.

He paused for a moment to reflect upon the reasons that he had accepted such an arduous task at his age. Money had nothing to do with it, to be sure. He had, in fact, entertained the idea of permanent retirement for more than a year now. But he could not quite figure out what to do with his time.

For some fifty years, he had carried the burden of time upon his reluctant shoulders. He had thrown himself into work and various projects. He read voraciously and wrote prodigiously, all in the effort to expel from his consciousness the incessant ticking of that cosmic clock.

With permanent retirement would come the anxiety of heavy moments laid end to end: the gazing out of windows on autumn afternoons, the recollections of fields and leaden skies, visions of another world, of another time…now, and forever, ash.

Truth was, Isaac had become indifferent to the rolling wheels of the world out of painful necessity. Being around the vibrancy of youth and laughter bordered on the unbearable. Now there was little vitality left in reserve to carry him through the winter years of retirement. He would settle into the background of these rooms like a piece of dusty furniture.

And because of his self-imposed exile from his neighbors, there would be a harvest of loneliness to reap as well. So there was little reason for him not to work …not to continue until sickness or death came for him.

"Enough," he thought aloud. "Time to put it in gear, Isaac." He assumed a false interest and prepared for the task at hand.

—— ✶ ——

He arrived in Atlanta in the late afternoon. "The Belle Epoch," he told the questioning eyes in the taxi's rearview. It was a long ride from the city's perimeter to its heart. The home rush was on and the traffic was locked in a slow crawl past the campus of Georgia Tech. Isaac leaned back in the air-conditioned cocoon and closed his eyes.

There was never any homesickness when his work called him out into the world. That Boston brownstone was mostly a place to store his things: a mantle for his pictures, a room of shelving for his books…a fireplace to stave off winter's increasing chill. What home he still possessed he carried in his heart. As the cab's motion lulled him, he could see her, running toward him in that summer dress that filled and burst his heart. She took his hand and pulled him down into the tall grass. The field was a lover's field. And they were very much at home. She loosened his shirt as he kissed at the hollow of her soft throat, and murmured against her skin, "Lessa, Lessa…"

"Hey, sport. You OK back there?"

The questioning eyes in the mirror that see only an old man in a fit of sleep, speaking in the tongue of ancient memories.

"Yes. I just dozed off. I'm fine."

"Do you always speak foreign languages in your sleep?" the driver inquired.

Isaac frowned. "Only when I dream."

Isaac settled into his room, ordered the paper and a bottle of Sancerre, and made a few calls. He maintained business acquaintances across the country, and during his assignments he would place short courtesy calls to inquire of his associates' health and families. It was strictly professional, a part of his travel habit that included a daily investigation of the obituaries to look for familiar names.

The wine arrived and he poured himself a tall glass, declining the steward's services. He tilted the bowl against the light and watched the facets leap across the tight surface of the straw-colored liquid. As the wine opened, he walked slowly around the room, inhaling the subtle notes of hay and grapefruit. He lowered himself into a chair, scanned the paper, and finished two glasses of the heady summer wine.

After a warm shower he walked out onto the balcony and gazed across the city's horizon. He had mixed feelings about Atlanta. There were certainly more hospitable southern cities. Atlanta had become a transient town, pulling its population from around the country and across the globe. One of those places which few of the inhabitants were actually "from." In an attempt to be a little of everything for everybody, she had lost some of what southern charm she had managed to resurrect from Sherman's punitive arson.

It was Savannah that still retained the Georgian grace. But what Atlanta did have going for her was a kind of blunt-force tolerance that had been hard-won in the struggle for Civil Rights. Many a beating had been taken upon many courageous shoulders, and many of those heroes had come from the poorest quarters of Atlanta. Money and the working class didn't mix much in class-conscious Atlanta even now, but no matter your color or sexual preference, you could walk with head high in Hotlanta today. And she did have one hell of a skyline.

He decided to take the last of the failing sun and stroll for a bit. It was now dusk, and the city was wrapped in that peculiar blue-gray garment that all southern cities wear at that time of evening. A Confederate twilight that would soon surrender to an early moon.

He turned east onto a less-populated sidewalk and walked headlong into the leafy, emerald-dusk of Piedmont Park. It had been several years since he had visited the city, and this park had been a favorite spot in which to take his crowded thoughts for a stroll. But there was a difference now. Like so many urban parks around the country, there was an air of neglect, careless litter, and the aimless shuffling of the homeless. He was immediately overcome by a vagrant melancholy.

The homeless were scattered about like an encamped army awaiting some phantom order. There was a vast anonymity. The scene conjured sharp and immediate memories. As a former refugee who had shuffled through the camps after World War Two, Isaac knew the formless, faceless mob, and their detachment from the world even here, in the midst of a great city.

Where did these people come from? What had detoured them from the wide boulevard of what they had longed to be onto this dead-end street of what they had become? There was no evidence of will. He found it ironic that this state of non-attachment, this submersion of the will, was in fact the high-ground sought by mystics and sages the world over. But for these people it was only the slow-footed grind of life on the mean streets. There was nothing holy about it. This was not the land of the enlightened.

He was mesmerized and walked deeper into the gathering darkness of the park. Past a long row of benches, each now occupied by a supine figure, claiming territory in the simple act of lying down now that the play and the leisure of the living had vacated the lawns. He looked closely at each of them, wondering at the whisper-thin line between them and himself.

On the last bench in the row, removed from the others by a small group of trees, he saw an elderly woman lying on her back, wrapped in several layers of worn clothing and the fetid odors of urine and alcohol. She was clutching a ragged flop doll with mop-string hair to her breast. Isaac glanced down at her, then hastened to move past the wretched figure when he caught part of a phrase from the lullaby she was singing.

He glanced around, then edged closer to the woman so that he might hear her words more clearly. She took no notice of him, lost as she was in the sweet escape of precious memories. Now he could discern her words all too clearly.

"Hush little baby, don't say a word.

Daddy's gonna but you a mockingbird.

And if that mockingbird don't sing…"

Isaac flinched away from her, her words too close to his own recurring dreams. It almost seemed a cruel hoax but for the undeniable poverty of this creature on the bench. He reached out a hand to touch her hair, lightly, not wishing to disturb her reverie, but acknowledging a sublime thread between them.

He rose and turned away, swallowing hard and already captured by the haunt of her. This casual encounter would never leave him. But he was going to leave this park. Right now.

Retracing his steps, and walking quickly now among the full bruise of the deepening shadow, it occurred to him that he had officially entered "the wrong place at the wrong time."

What in the world was he doing? Hadn't seven and a half decades of life taught him anything? Why not just hang a sign on his back, preferably in neon, "I am an old and desperately helpless fool with a rather large sum of money in my pocket. Which way to the cleaners?"

There were only a hundred yards to the street; no need to panic. But he would have to remember to give himself a stern talking-to when he got back to the bright security of his room. And maybe a shot of Drambuie.

He was just beginning to loosen up, smiling at the carelessness that had gotten him into this situation, when one of the shadows that crowded the path up ahead detached itself and began to move deliberately in his direction.

Several varieties of bells and klaxons sounded in his head. He hadn't felt such a keen awareness of danger in nearly fifty years. His feet came to a halt on their own, neither wanting to advance nor finding the will to turn and flee.

The figure approached, and Isaac's apprehension grew. "Calm down," he told himself. "It's only a man out for a walk in the park. He is probably as uncomfortable as you are."

But he knew without question that it wasn't true. There was something supremely confident in the way the stranger strode the dark path. Something powerful, and sinister. Isaac was in trouble.

As the stranger drew parallel to his paralyzed position, Isaac was suddenly engulfed by the conflicting energies of sympathy and great indifference. He turned to face the man, half expecting an introduction. And for one spiked and icy moment, Isaac saw his error. The dense veils of reality parted and something unnatural peered through. He felt as though he had taken a blow to the forehead and stepped backward to steady himself. Just as abruptly, the world regained its orbit as the man moved on, leaving a dozen questions lingering in the air behind him. Isaac glanced back just once, but the figure had already moved beyond the spectrum of light. Isaac hurried back to his suite.

That night as he lay in bed, fingers laced behind his head, he allowed his thoughts to return to the incidents in the park. Oddly enough, it was easier for him to dismiss the bizarre encounter with the stranger than it was the memory of the old woman on the bench.

The poor woman was caught in, and represented, the vein-like webs of a life that gathered in the gossamer corners of his dark memories. The shadowed places that he sought to avoid had been thrust once more before his eyes. There was nothing to be done now but close those eyes and allow her to come to him.

Down and back, he floated through the misty sorrows of his years. It was so bittersweet to be back home, again…

He was a boy, running through the sparse woods on the outskirts of Warsaw. Twelve years old, free and sun-warmed as he darted between the trees. He was going to see his uncle, as he did every Saturday. It was his favorite part of the week. Aunt Ruth would have made hamentaschen or Rugelach cookies. And if Uncle Jonah wanted to ramble on about Theodor Herzl, as he often did, then the day would still be salvaged down at the creek, by the tug of a fish at the end of his line.

He veered from the path and dashed down the steep bank of the creek, running hard now, gathering speed for the final sprint to his uncle's house. Suddenly he pulled up hard and stopped in his tracks. There was a voice coming through the woods, not far off…though it might as well have come from Heaven. It was sweeter than Aunt Ruth's pastry, a completely new appreciation for him. The sound of a young girl singing.

He followed the voice down through the foliage along the banks. There on a slab of rock jutting out into the stream, singing one of her own lullabies to a doll, was the 14-year-old poet, Lessa Frankle. He stood above her behind a tree, like a dumbstruck animal, as something in her voice punctured him like tender thorns.

"My sweet child
You are lucky, indeed.
Papa will take care
Of all your needs. My husband
Keeps us both from harm,
And holds back the night
With two strong arms…"

When she had finished her song, Isaac walked down to her and tried to introduce himself. But her voice had rendered his mute. So she talked to him until he finally found his voice. By that time he never wanted to hear any words but hers, ever again.

They became the thickest of thieves and the finest of friends. In their innocence, they shared everything. School work, holidays, walks in the rain, and bathing in the creek on sultry summer days. By the time their families realized that they had grown older and ever closer, it was far too late to think of chaperones and traditional courtship. In any case, events were shaping that captured everyone's attention in much more alarming ways.

The beds in this hotel had always been some of Isaac's favorites when he traveled. But on this night they might as well have been made of car radiators and rusty springs. He crossed and uncrossed his feet, willing himself to relax. He didn't want to pursue these memories any further. There was a deadline, and work to focus on. Memories of Lessa, indulged and embraced, would only be an unhealthy distraction.

He tossed on the sheets for another hour but sleep had no mercy for him. He staved off memories of Lessa in one context only to find her waiting for him in another. The image of the refugees returned to him and, sighing deeply, he surrendered once more to the sweeping current of his thoughts.

It was late summer, 1945, and Isaac had been blown across the European continent like a ragged flag, seeking some word, some small sign of Lessa's existence. He had traveled with great hardship to all the major refugee camps, and had witnessed the crowded squalor of the Jerusalem-dreamers. Hundreds and thousands waiting to become the flesh and bones of the new promised land.

Eventually he made his way to London. The British were the administrators for the majority of the camps, and he had come to examine their records. It was there, as his hope broke in waves of despair over the vague and fruitless files, that he met the young priest, Evan Connor. And thus began his slow, halfhearted revival with the human race.

Father Connor heard the outline of Isaac's story and took him into his home, where the tormented young Jew stayed for the next five months. The priest was patient and compassionate. Only Lessa could have salvaged Isaac's wounded spirit. In her absence, Isaac turned gradually to what he saw as a possible redemption in the Catholic tradition. He would now attempt to reconnect with a faith that had fled from him during the horror that was Auschwitz.

To Isaac, the God of Abraham had proven His cruel indifference by shrugging His shoulders as the swastikas danced around the pyre of Isaac's race. Father Connor spoke of the same God, but with a powerful difference that appealed to the dreams of the young survivor. Resurrection. Eternal life. If this were true, then Lessa might well be waiting for him out there beyond the veil.

Resurrection became his ideal. If this Jesus really was the personification of eternal love, then there was at least a possibility that he would see his wife again. And a possibility was all that Isaac needed to subscribe.

It wasn't as huge a leap as he might have imagined. When he approached Father Connor with the idea of Conversion, the priest seemed more concerned with the implications than Isaac did. He invited Isaac into the book-lined rectory and poured tea for them both. The silence balanced on a wire between them.

"How long have you been considering this, Isaac?" The priest broke the silence after several tense moments.

"For about two months now, Evan."

"And what, exactly, do you believe that Catholicism is going to mean in your life? Especially in light of all that you have been through these last few years?"

Isaac broke the priest's hard gaze and looked down at the floor. That was a very focused and somewhat unsettling question. How could he explain about Lessa? What could he possibly say that would make sense to a man who had never lain with a woman?

Who had never experienced that peculiar fusion of body and soul? Even under these circumstances he knew that he couldn't begin to unravel his truest feelings for the sake of the priest's questions. The gravity of love's loss was still too heavy upon his tongue. But a substantial part of it would *have* to be said. This wasn't a new suit of clothes he was trying on. His love depended on it. And his hope commanded it.

He raised his eyes again and met those of the priest with a steady gaze.

"Let me ask *you* some questions, Evan. What is God? Is He supreme love, as the words of Christ suggest? Or is He brutally indifferent, as my people's most recent history implies? Does He hold conjugal love in as high a regard as He holds the love of compassion…the love that you and your brothers and sisters in faith have taken vows of celibacy for?"

The priest looked a little perplexed by Isaac's line of questioning. He had covered a lot of ground during conversion discussions, but this was a novel path. Isaac pushed more questions into the uncertain silence, his passionate motives flowing out of him.

"I want to know if God recognizes, and gives some sort of priority to, the love between a man and a woman who wanted nothing less than forever. Because if He doesn't, I am never going to see my wife again. And I could never want to know, or try to love, a God who would give us the capacity for such longing only to viciously rip the heart out of the dream. If there is no reunion to hope for, He can send me straight to Hell right now and skip the formalities."

Isaac's eyes blazed with accusation, with ten lifetimes' worth of anguish. Until now he had kept the depth of that suffering to himself. The world of men was no longer a place of meaning for Isaac Bloom. His attention was now focused on the afterlife, and the love that might yet await him there. Evan Connor was caught in that powerful undertow.

This truly was a soul in need. Here was a man who might never hope again. It was thin ice for a young priest to skate out upon. But there was great possibility here as well. And the priest had to believe that God was trying to reveal something to both of the young men who sat pondering the eternal in a London rectory, only months removed from the greatest carnage in "civilized" history.

"Isaac, I can't even begin to comprehend your pain. And I certainly can't offer any simple answers to your questions. I will say this: When love and faith come together, it is the most powerful combination imaginable. I have seen lives changed and great miracles performed under such circumstances. It is as though God takes our abilities and multiplies them. But the best product of this rare confluence is an unshakeable inner peace. A peace that is everlasting. That is, it lasts as long as one's faith does. Your own faith has been sorely tested. But your love, at least in the most perfect conjugal sense, has stood firm. We need to set about the recovery of your faith."

Isaac leaned back into his chair and sighed deeply. "That alone could constitute a miracle," he thought bitterly.

During the course of the next several months, the two men were nearly inseparable. They took long afternoon walks through Hyde Park and along the Thames. Through autumn leaves and over wintered bridges. One step at a time.

Father Connor spoke of the risks of faith, and of justified hope. He took the great historical lessons of suffering and put them into a personal context...always bringing the conversation back around to love.

He was an enthusiastic teacher, learning as much from his own ideas as he hoped Isaac was. He tried to convey to Isaac that the great mining-out of the heart that suffering performs could eventually be filled with the deepest kind of love—the kind that Isaac was on a quest to find—and that he would need faith if he were to realize the dream of eternity with his wife.

"Suffering often produces hatred and anger. But perhaps its greatest miracle is the softening of the heart...and that softening is love, Isaac."

Finally, two weeks before Easter of 1946, Evan Connor told his friend that he would administer the sacraments of baptism, confirmation and First Communion on Holy Saturday. Isaac spent the next twelve days in prayer, imploring St. Jude, the patron saint of Lost Causes, for intercession. He pleaded with all who would listen to preserve his marriage forever.

It was an evening ceremony. The church shadows danced in the flickering candlelight as Isaac made his way to the altar to receive his First Communion. Father Connor smiled at him and leaned forward to whisper in his ear.

"Rejoice, Isaac! I have been praying very earnestly for something to bring you comfort. I have never heard of this being done, but I can find no misgivings in my heart for what I am about to do. I have come to believe that Lessa's spirit does dwell within you as part of your own soul."

With that, the priest took *two* hosts, dipped them into the crimson wine, and held them forth like an answered prayer to Isaac's trembling lips.

"The body and blood of Christ."

From that time forward, whenever he received communion from Father Connor, he received it for himself and for Lessa. It may have been nothing more than a well-intentioned placebo for the ailing soul, but to Isaac it was the recovery of some measure of hope. Life would always be a sentence to be carried out as long as he was separated from his love, but now a possible pardon seemed to exist, out there somewhere.

In 1953, Father Connor was transferred to a parish in Boston. Isaac had stayed on in London after his conversion, and had found work with a major newspaper. When his one true friend departed, he could find no reason not to join him in America. By following

Evan to Boston, he could continue his faith, with the unique incentive of the two hosts.

Now, as memories finally gave way to fatigue, Isaac shifted onto his side, wrapped his arms around a pillow, and called out the day's final yearning.

"Lessa, come to my dreams. Please, come to me..."

Chapter Two

Isaac rose early the following morning, determined to focus on the task at hand and to put the previous night quickly behind him. Eleven cities needed to be covered in the next twenty-four days. There was no time for nocturnal involvement with dreams and ghosts...or strangers in the shadows.

He worked with intensity and by lunchtime he was famished. Last night's encounter was a thing of fading anxiety. He placed an order for a bottle of Pouilly-Fume and grilled chicken salad to be delivered to his room. He sat at the balcony table enjoying the brilliance of the cobalt sky and opened the paper, automatically, to the obituaries. No familiar names. He was just about to turn to the redundancy of the headlines when something caught in the smoky webs of reluctant memory and demanded his attention.

He glanced back over the obits and there it was, the vague little paragraph that marked the end of a life...and the end of a lullaby.

> Jane Doe. Unidentified elderly vagrant female.
> Found dead in Piedmont Park. Cause of death
> Unknown. Pending autopsy.
> Police do not suspect foul play.

Isaac rose and walked to the balcony's edge. He looked out over the rooftops and the busy streets toward Piedmont Park. He could see the density of trees that marked the park's interior. Dark questions of coincidence whispered like a rustle of leaves.

"Hush little baby, don't you cry..."

He knew it was her. That pitiful wraith, singing herself to sleep on a park bench, would dream no more.

Did the stranger in the shadows have anything to do with it?

"Careful, Isaac. There's a whole neighborhood of well-wishers back home just waiting for you to start chasing demons when you're out in the yard with that broom," he thought aloud.

In fact, his own fear deterred him as well. He knew that he had an over-active imagination. He was a writer, for Chrissakes. There were times, especially during recollections of the camp, that he doubted if he would return to the world intact. Best not to ponder what is unseeable, and unknowable.

But the question refused to die that easily. He had shared a bond with that old woman. He crossed himself and offered a prayer.

"Give her a good home, lord. And a soft pillow, free of tears."

—— * ——

The next day he caught a flight to Charlotte. By charging into his assignment, he was able to keep that old sorrowful ghost at bay. But that night, as he lay his head on the scented pillows, he was forced to succumb and invite her into the crowded haunts of his memory.

Over the course of the next several nights a pattern developed, in which his memories oscillated between the homeless woman and his wife. Lessa seemed especially close now, almost reproving in her love. His conscience was curiously co-mingled with thoughts of how Lessa would deal with recent events.

"There is nothing I can do for her, Mrs. Bloom," he would say to an empty chair. "She is at peace now," he would remark to the clothes in the closet. "This is ridiculous," to the bidet.

But still he could not free himself of the troubling idea that the old woman and the dark stranger were connected. And the notion that he should somehow get involved began to wear on his nerves.

Nine days later he was in St. Louis and lack of sleep was taking its toll. He didn't carry fatigue well, and when he checked in to the hotel the manager, who had known Isaac for a decade, politely inquired of his health. Isaac went straight to bed and into a dreamless sleep. When his call came at eight the next morning, he was already up and alert, feeling much renewed.

He ordered eggs Benedict, sourdough toast, and French press coffee, then stood for fifteen minutes under a scalding shower. When breakfast and the morning paper arrived he was feeling as frisky as a fifty year old. He avoided the obituaries for the moment, unwilling to dampen his mood with the news of death. The deceased were interred there in their little columns. They weren't going anywhere.

He read through the news and shook his head. "What have we become?" He gazed up at the ceiling and wondered aloud at the cruel and violent obsessions of mankind, and suddenly felt fatigue wash over him again. He sat there, half a century removed from the butchery of the Holocaust, and had to admit that the species hadn't learned a thing. He had avoided the obituaries, but why? Every newspaper in the world had become one redundant obituary for the planet, and for the most overrated species ever residing upon it.

With disgust, he turned at last to those neat little rows of the dead to look for any familiar names. All that remained of a life, of loves and disappointments. A name, whispered among friends, wept over by family...and called out in anguish in the long night of mourning.

Consciously he tried to avoid it, but his eyes kept returning to a troubling little paragraph that whispered of Atlanta.

> Itinerant male found dead
> near Braintree Station.
> Identity unknown. Cause
> of death uncertain.
> Pending coroner's report.

There was absolutely nothing to connect the two deaths. Nothing except a fevered imagination fueled by too many sleepless nights. He knew that he needed more rest than he had been getting. He also knew that he had taken the old woman's death too personally. He knew that the whole thing was crazy. He picked up the phone and got the number to the County Coroner's office.

—— ⋆ ——

"Sorry to keep you waiting, sir. Please follow me."

Isaac was led down several winding corridors of tile and chrome and flickering fluorescent lighting. The attendant introduced Isaac to the assistant coroner as Arthur Stratton, the name that he had given over the phone when he had called as a concerned relative looking for his missing brother.

Isaac was still swimming in disbelief over his own actions. He could not rationally explain to himself what he was trying to accomplish by viewing the dead body of a transient in a town that wasn't even his home. But when he tried to disengage himself from the gruesome task, he could feel the annoying tug of his conscience urging him on. He had to follow his gut on this if he was going to have any peace.

"Hello, Mr. Stratton. I'm sorry to meet under such solemn circumstances. Hopefully, this part of your search will prove futile."

The assistant turned and led the numbed Isaac to a gurney occupied by a linen-swathed figure. With no preamble, he pulled the pale garment from an even more colorless body.

The abrupt face-to-face with death caused Isaac to sway and clutch at the gurney for support, find the cadaver's arm instead, and pull it off the edge. It dangled there, outstretched with rigor mortis and pointing at the shaken old man like an accusation.

The attendant grabbed him and Isaac composed himself enough to notice the bruised and punctured skin near the joint of the dead man's elbow. The young coroner rearranged the arm, covered the face, and looked questioningly into Isaac's face.

Isaac finally managed to tear his gaze from the figure. He looked into the coroner's eyes and shook his head. "Just out of curiosity," casually, cautiously, "how did he die?"

"Nothing terribly exciting. A combination of poor physical health and morphine. I hesitate to call it an overdose because, in a healthy man, it wouldn't have been. But his body had deteriorated enough from the disease that would have eventually killed him that the drug in his veins was just enough to help things along."

"The disease that would have killed him?' Isaac asked, confused.

"Yes. It seems that he was only a few months from succumbing to throat cancer. He probably knew his time was short. The morphine must have offered a combination of escapes...from the pain, and from the reality of his condition."

They had returned to the lobby. The coroner was shaking his head. "Unfortunately, he is just one of many such stories around here. He won't even be missed. Well. I wish you luck in locating your brother, Mr. Stratton. Good afternoon."

Isaac had kept the taxi waiting, and his bags were in it.

"Take me to the airport," he said to the back of the driver's head.

He had anticipated something strange...almost a premonition. He had packed and made reservations on the next flight to Atlanta. This was a detour from his assignment, but he would only need a day there to wrap this up...whatever this was. Either there were similarities in the two deaths, or there weren't. He would give the matter just that much attention and no more. But that much was necessary if he was going to exorcise the nagging demons of his conscience.

Another call from a "concerned relative" got him access to Jane Doe's file, all that was left of her. One of several receptionists in the coroner's office pulled the particular Jane from the particular day in question and, without the slightest inquiry, handed the slender file over to him. He took a seat in the barren lobby and opened the folder to the two-page autopsy and coroner's report.

He read it through three times, then set it on the seat beside him. A tingling sensation started somewhere behind his eyes and spread rapidly to the base of his skull. This was not real. He was having a dream. The tingling ran like electric wires down both of his arms, straight through to each fingertip. A secretary coughed behind the counter. A phone was ringing.

It was a replay of the case in St. Louis, just a different potentially-fatal disease robbed of the chance to finish her off. Leukemia. And morphine.

He rose and returned the file to the receptionist, then walked stiffly to the exit and out onto the busy street. For several minutes he stood, blinking against the sun before returning to the counter and asking for a phone. He called a cab and went directly to the same hotel from which he had started upon this odyssey. In his room, he downed four quick shots of brandy and stretched out on the bed to think.

"Now what?" he asked himself pointedly. "Do I call the police? Excuse me, officer, but I was walking in Piedmont Park after dark and noticed a rather suspicious character. I believe he may have had something to do with the death of that homeless lady."

"Is that so? You were walking in the park after dark, saw a strange person and a homeless lady that you know was dead the next day? We'll check right into that, Mr…uh, what was your name again, sir?"

Probably not a great idea. Not yet, anyway. Better to do just a little more research on the subject. Then perhaps an anonymous call with all the facts laid out for the authorities. That seemed like an acceptable solution. He rolled onto his side, turned off the bedside lamp, and waited for sleep.

The next day he returned to the coroner's office, dealt with a different clerk, and used his real name and credentials to gain access to five years' worth of Jane and John Doe files. To the "why do you need this stuff?" question, he simply replied that he was conducting some research for a possible article on the homeless, and needed some baseline data that might indicate dietary habits, life expectancy, causes of death, etc.

He copied everything before returning to St. Louis that evening, where he repeated his request at that coroner's office the following day.

Files and photocopies were scattered about the suite. Before he examined any of them, he ordered a bottle of Secco-Bertani, ran a hot bath, and eased into the steaming tub to open the pores of his heart and mind to the problem before him. He had felt from the beginning that Lessa was somehow exerting a kind of psychic influence in this affair. He was not going to close his mind to that possibility. Rather, he would try even harder to tap in to her love and compassion. He would need her help to look bravely and objectively upon those files.

He took a long, fulfilling draw of the elegant wine and closed his eyes...soft cherries and strawberries, caressed by a firm acidity. Lovely. He took the mental notes for his travel piece, then cleared the present from his mind and allowed his thoughts to carry him back. Back through the smoke and thunder of his pain...and back, slowly. Until, at last, he could part the heavy, dark curtain that he kept sealed against Warsaw.

He and Lessa were at a popular night spot in the Stare Miasto, old Warsaw. It was a gay evening, warm and alive with stars. They were out with a group of friends: the young, the brave, and the creative heart of the city. They were dancing, and raising glasses to their esoteric little society.

Josef Griter, a longtime admirer and would-be lover of Lessa's, had just completed a satirical speech on the morally-enlightening qualities of Scotch whisky. Isaac took Lessa's hand and led her out to dance. With his arms safely around her, Lessa was able to let go of the last wisps of the anxiety that had clouded her days of late.

Isaac felt her relax into him and marveled again at how well they fit together.

"Josef will probably go to his grave carrying your heart on his sleeve," he said casually.

"Isaac. You exaggerate. Josef likes the idea of love more than he likes the work required to sustain it. He's too sentimental. And he admires every woman he knows he can never have. But he doesn't care for me any more than he cares for Sarah, or Judith. Besides, he loves you like a brother."

"Perhaps. But he would certainly jump at the opportunity to love you like more than a sister."

"You're jealous," she laughed against his shoulder.

"Of course I am. It goes with the territory of loving the most beautiful fish in the sea. One is always looking out for hungry sharks."

She squeezed his hand as they laughed some more, and laid her head against his chest. This was where she belonged. Her home was right here. And everyone who saw them together knew it. The song ended and they returned to the crowded table.

"Oh, Lessa! You've returned in the very nick of time." Josef took her hand from Isaac's and led her to the head of the table, explaining, "Karl has been driving the spikes of his alleged poetry into our ears, and we need you to soothe our fevered brains with something cool and embraceable. Ladies and, ahem, gentlemen," he shouted above the din at the table, "I give you the most lovely, the most talented, and temporarily the most obscure poet in all of Poland: Lessa Frankle! Or should that be 'Bloom'?" He winked knowingly at Isaac as the group applauded and whistled.

Lessa smiled and looked at each of her friends in turn. "These are the best of times," she thought. "But they cannot last."

She pushed the troubling whispers aside and addressed the table.

"You honor me with your enthusiasm. And Isaac has promised me that the ones who whistled will be entitled to a little extra over what was discussed."

Isaac pretended to reach for his wallet as everyone whistled in unison.

"I'm afraid that I have nothing new to share with you. I am working on some new pieces now, but they won't be finished for a while..."

The exaggerated agony of their pleas assailed her. "Anything, Lessa! Recite one of your lullabies."

She laughed. A luxurious and rich low-note melody. To Isaac, her laughter was her greatest lullaby.

She was enjoying herself, and smiled at them all again.

"All right, then. A lullaby for my sleepy friends.

As you fall to sleep now,
Remember to dream.
The night is not as long
As at first it seems.
The daylight needs its rest as well.
So use these hours between the suns
To laugh and sing in a sweet-dream spell.
Love finds its courage
In the shadows and shade,
Where it meets the monsters
That our selves have made.
But I will be here
When you've journeyed through.
(From the loving womb,
To the powerless tomb)
My candle burns all night for you."

They applauded furiously, offering her imaginary garlands and awards. A hasty crown was fashioned from a napkin and placed upon her head. Isaac burned with love. She walked quickly to his end of the table and sat next to him. He kissed her ear.

"Have I mentioned that I love you?"

She looked into the fountain-brightness of his eyes.

"Oh, Isaac. You tell me in all the words you speak and in all the things you do. And you give me such courage."

She squeezed his hand hard. The two of them sat there, but somewhere else, as the Warsaw night played out around them.

There were more drinks and more stories, and the talk gradually turned from the lightness of lullabies to the heavy rhythms of Germany and Hitler.

Karl had gotten a little drunk, and was speaking with too much fervor, too much false bravado, as though he would rally all of Poland to his words.

"Hitler's eyes rattle around in his head like the roulette balls at the casino. Where will they land? Italy? Austria...Poland? Not Poland, my friends. Poland will fight! But Austria will roll over like a kicked dog. That is where the little madman will go to expand his beloved Bavaria."

"Poland may well put up some resistance. But it won't be for or about you, dear Karl." Patrik joined in after not saying two words to anyone except Judith all night. "You are not a Pol to the Pols. You are a bargaining chip. To be used if the madman becomes bored with the stakes and wants to play a different kind of game."

Karl's eyes shifted nervously about the group, seeking some support. Patrik was the understated voice of brutal truth, and Karl still preferred the comfort of lies.

"Game? You speak of games. But I am a Pol. My family helped build this city. We are, all of us, Pols together. And we will stand shoulder to shoulder against Hitler's ambitions."

Patrik stood and gathered his things and the hand of Judith, then looked at Karl as he passed from the group. "You are a Jew, Karl. You will believe what you must so that you can sleep at night. But don't sleep too soundly, brother. The wolves are on the prowl."

Patrick and Judith departed as Karl turned his pleas on the remaining clique. Lessa grabbed at Isaac's arm, layers of panic in her eyes.

"Take me home, Isaac. I've heard all of this over and over again. It's everywhere we go."

Isaac had seen this fear in her before. He knew better than to try to assuage it in the middle of someone else's discourse on the subject. He rounded up their things and they slipped out, unnoticed by all except Josef.

He put his arms around her as they walked away from the crowds and the noise. As he had so often in the recent past, he set about the task of comforting her against her dismay.

"It is all a bunch of gossip and empty talk, Lessa. No one takes Hitler as seriously as they pretend to. He makes for great conversation, but he isn't a monster."

"I fear that is exactly what he is. He is the entire topic of discussion at the university. His speeches are passed around and read aloud in the halls. He even has supporters right here in Warsaw. His speeches scare me, Isaac. I want to leave Warsaw. I want us to go from here together. There is a darkness gathering that the human race has not yet imagined."

"Lessa! You have allowed nightmares into your head that have no basis in fact. Besides, where would we go? Our families, our friends, and our work are all here. This has been the home of our families for generations. It makes no sense to run from someone's words."

"It does if those words are applauded by an entire nation." She stopped and turned to face him squarely. "He has his country believing in the things he says. He could tell them that the moon was green and they would listen. He has revived their national pride and honor at the expense of several scapegoats, including our own people. And he has the army and industrial base to go wherever and whenever he wants. He terrifies me. I have the most horrible dreams."

He put his arms around her again, drew her close, and once more felt the tension leave her. Somewhere up the street a lonely violin was weeping Albinoni's Adagio, and they began to move together, slowly. Few people passed them at this hour, and he waltzed her up the street to her father's house. She was calm again, and smiling.

"Love finds its courage in the shadows and shade," he reminded her. "Sing yourself to sleep, my beauty. My candle is burning for you. I will see you in the morning."

He kissed her hungrily and felt her body sigh.

"Goodnight, Isaac," she murmured into his mouth.

"Goodnight, Lessa," he murmured back.

The bittersweet memory caught in the little whirlpool over the tub's drain and went round and round, finally disappearing. He had relived that night a thousand times. And at the zenith of her need he had changed it all...changing history. He had taken her in his arms and whispered fiercely, "Yes. Gather your things and we will go. If we are wrong, we will laugh at ourselves. And we can tell our children how foolish we were. It will be a humorous memory to grow old with."

But he hadn't changed history. He hadn't fled with her. And his memories were all that was left of Lessa. Memories rich with the attendant anguish of his failure.

He was a tired old man alone in the tub with his swirling troubles, a troubling task before him. He stood up and grabbed a towel, then walked back into the suite to begin.

CHAPTER THREE

Five hours later, the phone interrupted his immersion in homeless mortality. It was his editor.

"For God's sake, Isaac, it's been a major bitch tracking you down! What are you still doing in St. Louis? You were supposed to be in Baton Rouge two days ago. You're going to have to hustle now because the deadline has been moved up by three days. Are you catching this, Isaac? Isaac?"

"And good evening to you, Adam. Yes, I am quite well, thank you for asking. I will leave for Baton Rouge tonight. And I will finish the piece on time, as usual. Not to worry. Bon soir, Adam."

He hung up with the editor's strangled reply choking to escape the mouthpiece.

Baton Rouge was a distraction to him right now. There was a subtle but startling pattern in those files, too much to cite coincidence. He had little faith in coincidence anyway. It seemed certain that someone was killing homeless people in Atlanta and St. Louis. The pattern dated back to the beginning of the five-year period that he had access to. One or two people, always afflicted with life-threatening illness, and morphine. It maintained a cycle that repeated itself at roughly-annual intervals.

It was easy to see why the authorities hadn't noticed anything amiss. The police, when they bothered at all, only dealt with the homeless in their own towns. They would be oblivious to similar deaths in other parts of the country. And, after all, they were homeless people. There was no one to miss them. No one to demand an answer to suspicious questions. What was suspicious about unhealthy drug users living on the streets, anyway? For someone who enjoyed killing for killing's sake, this was an almost perfect paradigm.

In fact, there really was little reason for alarm. Not officially. If he hadn't had the disquieting encounter with the stranger in Atlanta, even he would have put this matter to bed days ago. But it was undeniable. There was something sinister and purposeful about that man. Wasn't there?

Or was it him? An old man, who had witnessed too much horror, jumping at shadows?

He had to slow down and think rationally. Perhaps Baton Rouge wasn't a distraction after all. If there was a pattern in the two cities he had already visited, it was possible that the pattern was in place elsewhere…in other southern cities.

Whatever the case, he would certainly need more information before he approached anyone else with his discoveries. If he was wrong, there was a world of implication for his future that he didn't care to think about.

"Come on, Lessa. Let's go see if our phantom has been busy in Baton Rouge…"

— ✶ —

"Good evening, Mr. Bloom, we've been expecting you. How was your flight?"

"Uneventful, Thom. My favorite kind. How have you and your family been getting on since I saw you last? That must be five or six years now."

"Just fine, sir. Thank you for asking. What can we do to make your stay more comfortable? Still fond of old Gevrey-Chambertins?" The concierge asked with a wry smile.

"I am still Chambertin's slave, Thom. Please have a bottle of the '85 sent up, and some chèvre. I'll order some dinner after I have settled in. And I'll need a taxi at ten in the morning. Thank you."

He made himself comfortable in his room. When the wine arrived, he poured a tall glass and turned the suite's stereo up, loud. It was Delibes, Lakme. Sensual, powerful, and thoroughly revitalizing.

"Well, Lessa," he spoke softly, "what do you think of this situation? Your husband can now add criminal detective to his resume. That is, if he should ever seek some honest labor."

He rose and began to walk around the four rooms of his suite, talking to her as he wandered.

"Why would anyone want to kill these people? Of all the victims to choose, these have the least to offer. Nothing at all for anyone to envy or lust after. Is it because they use drugs? Is someone killing them with their own poison…as some sort of revenge? And how did I get involved?"

Now there was a sixty-four dollar question. The man who didn't even pause for conversation on the streets of his own neighborhood was suddenly playing Sherlock Holmes halfway across the country.

But he had to admit, morbid circumstances aside, that he felt more vital and alive than he had in many years. Still, he wasn't going to get any more involved than was absolutely necessary. He would gather what information he could as discreetly as he could, confirm his theories as well as possible, and turn the entire matter over to the police.

He went through the rooms again, turning off all the lights. He turned the stereo's volume up another notch, so that he could hear it outside, and took his wine out onto the balcony.

The night was a brilliant sapphire with the lights of the city below him sparkling like facets in the gem. Dvorak drifted out to him now. He swirled the wine around and over his tongue, enjoying the heady sensuality. And, answering the call of his ever-present longing, Lessa was before him, laughing. It was no longer Baton Rouge. It was Warsaw, four nights before their wedding, 1938. He was teaching her to drink Cognac. She wasn't getting it, but she was certainly enjoying the lesson.

"Once more…no, no! Inhale *before* you swallow…"

"Pffffttt!!! She sprayed a mouthful across his shirt, and began to laugh and choke all at once. He thumped her on the back.

"All right, you lush, that's enough. You peasants are below refinement. This stuff is too good for you. Be off! You're banished to the potato stills!"

"No, Isaac! One more chance. I promise I'll get it right this time. Please? I'll be your best friend."

He laughed in spite of himself. "All right. One last time. A mouthful of the brandy, now inhale through your mouth so that the air mingles with the liquid, then swallow. And finally, exhale forcefully through your nose. OK? Try it."

"Yes, but you have to promise that you will kiss me as soon as I have done it. Promise?"

"Of course. That's easily done…if you're still standing. Now drink!"

She concentrated on each step of the process until she blew the air out of her nose like a surfacing cetacean. He applauded and laughed, then leaned into her lips, which she parted to allow the sip of Cognac that she hadn't swallowed to flow into his mouth. He swallowed it down and opened his eyes to look at her.

"Miss Frankle, I do believe that there will be severe reprimands when I return you to your father's house. You're drunk. And your kisses are making me so."

"If you liked that one, wait until Friday," she whispered teasingly.

He took her into his arms and ran his fingers through the blue-black night of her hair, kissing her over and over again until they were both gasping.

"I can't believe that you are going to be my wife. My wife! What did I ever do to deserve such a gift?"

"You have given me a life of love, Isaac. That is what you have done. And I intend to spend forever giving it back to you…

back to you

back to

you."

The Dvorak had become Chopin's Nocturnes, and the city blurred beneath him. There was not enough wine in the world… and not enough Cognac. Isaac went to his prayers and to his bed.

The next morning he took his taxi to the Parish Coroner's office, explained his "project," and was given the copied files that he requested. Now he really had a base to work with. If the pattern were revealed here in Baton Rouge, and if it surfaced in other cities that he would visit later, he would have plenty of evidence to hand over to the FBI.

It was a stunning thought, that this could somehow be a national phenomenon. Lord, maybe it was just a little too stunning. He sat down on one of the folding chairs in the lobby and quickly scanned through a handful of files. It didn't take long to find what he was looking for. And that fact bothered him greatly.

Could he really believe his eyes? Hadn't this all started with an old woman singing lullabies in the dark, which had somehow conjured images from his own past? It was a past that he had never truly been able to leave behind. What did that say for his objectivity?

He glanced around him at the handful of people in the lobby. That middle-aged woman with the permanent scowl…would she see the same pattern? Would anything seem odd about sick and dying homeless people using too much morphine?

He had felt certain that he had stumbled onto something sinister. But this was starting to become unraveled and overwhelming. And the more involved he became, the more foolish he felt.

He fought the urge to abandon the matter right there and returned to his hotel to take a closer look. He sifted through the material carefully, methodically, taking his time. There was a growing fear that his own credibility would eventually come into question. After several exhausting hours, however, he knew that he was still involved. Whatever was happening in Atlanta and St. Louis had found its way to Baton Rouge as well.

His next stop would be New Orleans. From there it was on to Biloxi, Pensacola and Miami. It would require only a little extra effort to investigate the pattern in those cities. After that, if there was solid evidence, he would certainly wash his hands of all of it and hand it over to the professionals. He turned his attention to his assignment, then packed for his morning journey to one of his favorite cities: New Orleans.

Chapter Four

It was a short, pleasant drive from the Louisiana state capital to the good-times capital of the country. He had rented a car and, with the top and windows down, was pushing the speed limit through the glossy wetlands of the nation's delta.

The sunlight danced across Lake Pontchartrain, to the east, and all the way back, skipping off his windshield and diving out over the marshes to the west. Sprites and nymphs and laughing eudemons could be guessed at out there among the cypress roots and the Spanish moss. There was the fragrant knowledge of persuasive moons and eager, swollen waters. There was the pungent, olfactory reasonings of ancient decay.

A flight of herons dipped heavy blue wings along the silver surfaces and rose as one above the spillway, tacking along the brackish breezes in the direction of Good Hope.

Isaac was already falling victim to the spell that New Orleans casts well out beyond her suburban sprawl. It's forgotten now, but New Orleans was once much more than the Vieux Carre and the hard, tangled edges of Old Algiers. Her people brought things to her, to her center, from the darkly quiet places and the weathered faces of the delta. New Orleans was nothing less than a sassy, hungry, angel-whore spider that sat waiting at the sensitive, twitching middle of her web. Waiting for the edges to alert her to some new, old thing. When it arrived, she assimilated it right into her DNA. And there it mingled with all that is juicy...with all that is the very marrow of life. Like the blind, people wander towards her from all over, their arms outstretched and fingers splayed, reaching and yearning and longing for that mysterious and mystical essence.

He drove on, tripping the wires of Kenner and Metairie, then veered toward the river so that he could approach her heart from the oak-shaded avenues of the Garden District. Anticipation crackled in the wires above the clanging street cars and drifted on the sweet, high energy of the uniformed children who lined the tracks. Catholic kids, waiting for their school bus-trolleys, blowing the same sad-laughing notes that the city's children had blown since slavery.

Isaac caught the strains of music when he passed beyond the boundaries of industrial Baton Rouge. They grew more complex and inviting as he neared his destination. Jazz was the city's Siren Song, impossible to ignore. It issued and oozed and seeped from even—and especially—the poorest corners, from the most unlikely sources of sad, black passion. Subterranean longings moved her people along the streets and through the pot-holed mazes of ordinary life, pulsing like a rhythm, bringing roots up through the surface of the creative soils again and again, generation after generation. Jazz was the fermented fruit, the ever-fragrant flower that perpetuated itself from the moist, mossy earth of the city's dreams and disappointments.

It was Isaac's third encounter with New Orleans. He could not have prepared himself for what was to be revealed there.

His hotel was touristy, full of newlyweds and Midwesterners come south for a go-cup full of the taboo...something spicy to add to the doldrums of later and less-enthralling recollections. Isaac didn't bother to unpack before he was out again among the joyful crowds and hawking hustlers of the Big Easy.

He avoided Bourbon Street, savvy enough to save that experience for the perspective of the night. Instead, he wandered the consumer-Casbah of Royal St. Peering from the sidewalk into the dim shadows where stuffed gator heads and vintage Mardi Gras masks grinned back at him.

He enjoyed the blatant show-offiness of the place, and the inevitable sidewalk artists around Jackson Square. The shirt-sleeved crowds flowed around him, and shared his mood. It was a highly probable day.

In an hour he was among the Third World flavors and aromas of the French Market. A frown had lifted from his face somewhere back on St. Charles Avenue. Seeing the red and green awnings flapping in the lazy river breezes, and the way the merchants shared big, contagious smiles as they offered their savory peppers and sweet pralines, Isaac felt a bond with the species that he hadn't experienced in decades.

—— * ——

He had the desk reserve a table at Antoine's and dressed impeccably for dinner. A dove-gray suit, white broadcloth shirt, his favorite silk tie. Here was yet another reason to love this multicultural adventure of a city: people actually dressed for dinner. A gypsy-camp of locals would board the streetcars uptown, travel merrily along to Canal and walk (some would say sashay), from there into the Quarter. There would be strolling cocktails and random meanderings into music bars. Much later, they would stand in line outside of Irene's Cuisine, or the Napoleon House, or dozens of other exquisite culinary options, and the sidewalk party would commence until the maître d emerged to wave you in, like you had just won the gold ticket at Willy Wonka's. The others in line would smile like they were actually thrilled for you, and in a way they were, but they were equally envious and would down a couple more Sazeracs to mask their disappointment.

Isaac walked the few blocks from his hotel to St. Ann and entered the classic mirrored dining rooms of Antoine's. Antoine's had once been a destination for the disgraced Napoleon himself. But at the last hour the plans had fallen apart. The secret room at Antoine's remained vacant and Napoleon died in exile, never having tasted the excellent catfish coubillion that waited there, one full-sail ship's voyage away. To have died in exile AND to have missed out on Antoine's could only be considered a kind of double Hell, really.

Isaac dined on boudin and etouffee and washed it all down with a chilled Vouvray. By nine he was ready for the smorgasbord of dandy-shenanigans that New Orleans serves up on a nightly basis to her fortunate guests. In her warm embrace, every guest is a guest of honor.

He stood outside the cramped, packed confines of Preservation Hall and let the brass wash over him like a baptism. It was blatantly arousing. People jumped like startled voodoo-victims, slapping at the air, kicking at curbs, crying out the names of gods and strangers. Several of the tourists could be seen glancing furtively over their shoulders, like fugitives from monotony, half-expecting the authorities to arrive with bullhorns and rubber bullets and drag them, kicking and screaming, from the scene of excessive fun. The night was damp with sexy insinuation.

He had learned quickly that this was a city of perspectives. One was either observer or observed. Isaac knew that he would pay dearly in the morning, but he had jumped on the side of the fence where the grass was uncut, slightly littered, but oh-so-much greener.

At a couple ticks past two in the morning he glanced at his watch. Startled by the lateness of the hour, he headed off in the direction of the Café du Monde for some coffee and beignets before retiring. Great flowing crowds of curiosity still roamed the streets, with no sign of quitting them anytime soon. It reminded him of Barcelona, another passionate city where the adults felt blessed by fate and circumstance to have become characters in such an extraordinary, vibrant poem. The café was awash in Mississippi moonlight and the harmonies of several languages being spoken at once.

Cafe du Monde was a jovial catastrophe. The waitstaff was hopelessly outdone by the intoxicated revelry of the patrons. Men and woman in discolored aprons scurried about, refilling empty mugs and swiping at the collected confections that lay in snow-like drifts upon the tiny tables.

Isaac found a vacant chair at a table with three young women from the medical college of Tulane University. He knew this because they immediately introduced themselves as such. They too were showing the effects of a four-hurricane season. The women were taken with his manners, his attire, and his subtle accent, and decided to flirt with the elegant old man for fun. A well-groomed blonde in her mid-twenties reached across the table and touched his left hand.

"That is a beautiful ring. May I ask where you got it?"

Isaac, always suspicious of the motives of strangers, looked at her closely. She was strikingly attractive and obviously accustomed to the attentive responses of men. There was a corruption of cynicism in the deep pools of her emerald eyes.

"Certainly," Isaac said, smiling. "It was given to me by my wife on the day that I gave her its twin."

The blonde snorted and smiled back at him. "I assumed that it was a wedding ring. But you misunderstood my question. I meant, where was it purchased."

Isaac was already bored with the woman. But he was in the best spirits that he had enjoyed in years, so he humored her.

"It isn't from America. It was designed in Poland by my wife's father."

"It really is gorgeous. Would you mind if I looked at it?"

"I'm afraid that I don't remove it..." Isaac stated as he stretched his hand across the table for her inspection.

"Ooohh, not even for me? Not even for a minute?" she asked, winking.

He winked back at her. "Not even for a minute. But may I offer you another cup of coffee?"

The blonde stared coldly past his shoulder. One of the other women, a short, round, matronly girl with kind eyes, sensed the awkwardness of her friend's failed jibing and tried to change the mood.

"You have a little bit of an accent. Is Poland your home?"

Isaac swung his gaze to her question and smiled again.

"Yes. Poland was my home. I lived there until I was about your age. I was married in Warsaw. But I have been in America many years now."

"Have you ever been back?" the girl continued, trying to steer the conversation back to friendly ground.

"No. I have never been back."

There was something in the way he answered that touched a sobering chord in all of them. Their table assumed a silent thoughtfulness. Isaac felt his previous enchantment drain away from him. He raised his hand to signal the waiter. When he did, the blonde noticed the tattooed number on his wrist.

She knew what the number implied, and she wondered how much he would be willing to talk about. It wasn't every day that one had coffee with an honest-to-god Holocaust survivor. She smiled at him again and her voice took on sweet molasses tones.

"Excuse me, Mr., uh..."

"Please, call me Isaac."

"Excuse me, Isaac, but is your wife from Poland, too?"

"Yes, she was…waiter! May I have the check for this table, please?"

"Is she here in New Orleans with you?"

He glanced sharply at her poker composure. "No. She died in Poland."

"Was it very long ago?" The blonde refused to let the matter drop. Her friends began to fidget nervously.

"Not very long ago at all. About fifty years. Waiter!"

"Did she die in the camp that you were in?"

To the four of them, the entire city seemed to inhale sharply. No one dared even look at him except the woman who had asked the question. And she herself would have said later that the question seemed to come from someone else's mouth. Isaac stared at her for several agonizing moments as the three women writhed in shameful agony. Then he spoke with pointed iciness.

"Yes. My dear wife perished in Auschwitz. I assume that you have heard of the place? Perhaps you have read about the numbers of people who were murdered there? But I would wager that you have never given more than a curious piece of your attention to the matter. It is a luxury for your generation that you can look back upon the Holocaust with indifference. The subject is entertaining, at best. Like reading about the Titanic or the Hindenburg explosion. And now I sit before you, living history. The intellectual drama that this fact creates in you causes you to lose your dignity while insulting mine. Well, ladies, I pray that you never experience such horror except through your callous questioning. But if you would mature your spirit, if it is important for you to become human, then may I suggest you ponder on the meaning of the word 'empathy.'"

Isaac stood and drained the dregs of the bitter chicory.

"Good morning, ladies."

His mood plummeted as he walked back to his hotel. A gnawing melancholy he knew too well resumed its incessant feeding on the open wound of his heart.

"I am old and weak and my teeth have all fallen out. There is only the love of my wife connecting me to what I once was."

He reached his room and undressed for bed, then threw himself upon the mercy of sleep. But it wouldn't answer his need.

What had happened to the years? Wasn't it only yesterday that he and Lessa had lain in the field outside the city? He had only closed his eyes for a moment against the mounting fear, and when he had opened them, she was gone.

That field...and the tender passage of urgent time that they had spent there. It pulled him back now, and he was too weak, too consumed with self-pity, to fight against it...

It was a lover's field. And they were very much at home...Not far from where Isaac had first laid eyes on the young girl singing lullabies to a doll. They lay in the tall grass beneath a leaden sky. It was a warm, rain-threatened day, and a whisper of breeze murmured like a rumor among the far trees.

The blanket they were seated on offered the best of what she was able to scavenge from the old city...and some of the things that they were saving for better times. But Lessa had realized that this day might be the last of the "better times" for the foreseeable future. So there was the Macedonian wine that a cousin had brought back to Warsaw as a gift to her. A thin kabanosy sausage, smoked and spiced with caraway. Some Kasar cheese from Turkey that she had sliced from the wheel in her mother's pantry. And a crusty bread, still warm, from her uncle's bakery. The perfect picnic. A feast worthy of the lover's-table. And a feast all but ignored by hers.

Isaac had been morose for many days. Lessa knew his unspoken misgivings, and his guilt over not having taken her from Warsaw. For, now, the Nazis had occupied Poland and were encamped around the city. There was no escape, especially for the Jews. There was even darker gossip that concerned their people: the centralization of all Jews into one controllable area of the city, possibly the ghetto.

This had all had a profound impact on Isaac's mood. And Lessa had watched him change from a secure and confident young man into a troubled, fearful caricature.

But, in a strangely paradoxical twist, Lessa was no longer afraid. She watched as the breeze danced along the tops of the tall grass that concealed them and she identified with that freedom. She was basking in the warm memories of their wedding night.

That single night had fulfilled her as a woman and had empowered her with a confident courage. There was a new awareness to her life…an evolved understanding of the rooted connection of all things. She had come to realize the true nature, and the awesome power, of spiritual surrender. There was a shared vitality in allowing her self to be fully absorbed in her husband's self, and into the living, essential world in general. She was necessary. Even more than that, her *love* was necessary. From this perspective she was even able to see, with great wonder, how the ugliness and the beauty of the world fit so seamlessly together.

"We are so much a part of everything else," she had mused that night as Isaac slept beside her. "There is no beginning or end…to life, or to love…there are only different forms."

In learning this, she had learned to abandon her fear of the night.

She had wanted to awaken Isaac, to share her excitement. Life was precious. Each moment was weighted with significance, and love justified all hope. She had watched him sleeping and laid her head on the rise and fall of his slumber, listening to the strong, deep music of his heart. They sailed on gentle currents through the first night of their marriage.

But now Isaac was drifting from her. And she knew that it wouldn't help for her to say, "Love is eternal." This was something his heart was going to have to learn on its own. Still, she needed to find the words that would bring him back to the precious moments of Now.

"Darling," she had spoken softly. "Talk to me. Tell me what it is that has hold of your mind, and what is choking your heart."

Several minutes of unanswered silence passed before she propped herself on an elbow and spoke again.

"Isaac, don't you understand that by worrying so much over the future you are robbing us of this glorious present? We are here, now…alone and free in this field. I am right here, beside you, your wife, your friend. This day belongs to us. Oh please, Isaac, let us laugh and talk as we did not so long ago. Teach me things…"

"I can teach you nothing!" Isaac turned suddenly to face her, bitterness flowing out of him. "You knew long ago what we needed to do but I ignored it. And I have put you in danger. Don't look to me for guidance, Lessa. A husband is supposed to protect his wife, and I have only…"

She interrupted him quickly. "Isaac, you are wrong! You haven't put me in danger. If we are in danger, it is not through our own doing. We have always loved and looked after one another. This is far beyond our control. But believing in our love, and appreciating our precious time together, is not. Love will see us through this, I know it. Don't isolate yourself from me now. Don't beat yourself up with what-ifs and why-nots. I need you, Isaac."

He stared up hopelessly at the heavens. The clouds were swollen with rain, and his thoughts were like them. He wanted to tell her…he needed to say…"I'm so sorry…"

Suddenly the wind shifted, bringing the darker clouds toward them and pushing the stifling heat aside as they came. Isaac could smell the approaching rain beyond the trees and he rose to collect their things. But Lessa reached up to take his hand and pull him back down onto the blanket.

They looked into each other's eyes, each with their own desperate need. The first raindrops kissed their faces like tears as Lessa drew his lips to hers.

"Eden was never tame," she whispered into his open mouth.

Isaac pushed her back and grabbed two handfuls of her windblown hair as the storm unleashed itself. Her mouth tasted of wet urgency. And despite his melancholy he felt the familiar arousal for her sweeping over him like the warm wind. It was easier than anything deserved to be. The way she unzipped him and found him ready in her hands. It was easy the way he lifted her skirt above her waist...easy...exposing the very center of herself to his need. And the easiest part, merging with her and with the erotic rhythm of her hips, with the erotic rhythm of her sighs...filling her to the apex...So. Damned. Easy. Nothing had been that easy since.

And he hoped, as the warm rain fell unnoticed upon his back, that the darkness before them would be as light-foot quick as this pleasure, as this brief and terrible joy.

Lessa opened her mouth beneath him, tasting the rain, tasting the mercury-goodness of her life, tasting his very heart. With the rain washing over her upturned face, she allowed the tears to fall freely.

"Oh, Isaac," she prayed. "My sweet Isaac."

Isaac curled himself into a ball of prayerful agony. "Dear God! Release me from this Hell and forgive my failure. Please, lord. Return me to my Lessa."

He covered his head with pillows. Two hours later a certain sleep came, and a mercy from his memories.

—— * ——

The next morning found a woozy, weary Isaac at the New Orleans coroner's office, a cup of chicory in hand and some sixty-two files in front of him. He was welcome to them but he would have to make the copies himself. "And would you like a cup of coffee while you're working, darlin'?"

After an hour of copying and reading files as he worked, he realized that it was missing. There was no similar pattern here in New Orleans. He would take everything back to his room for closer scrutiny but, aside from a very random and insignificant similarity or two, there was nothing in common with the other cities. Nothing close to what was happening just upriver in Baton Rouge.

That was odd. Why was New Orleans different when it shared the proximity of the other affected cities? Isaac left the coroner's office and returned to his room. A closer inspection revealed nothing new.

"Well," he thought aloud, "tomorrow I'll be in Biloxi. We'll see what's happening there."

CHAPTER FIVE

Father Evan Connor left his residence and walked four blocks to his church. He entered the sacristy and prepared himself to receive confession. As he pulled the chasuble over his head he focused his thoughts on the sacrament that he was about to administer.

It had, of late, begun to mystify him…to stir his imagination at the power men had assumed. He was about to grant total absolution for a myriad of sins. And he would do it, as he had so many countless times in the past, in the name of God.

There would be a line of devout Catholics waiting for his blessing. For most of them, it was a powerful new beginning, an opportunity to start afresh. But for him it was, increasingly, redundant and pedantic. The same penance for so many different sins. Ten "Our Fathers"…five "Hail Marys"…or five "Our Fathers" and ten "Hail Marys"…or ten and a rosary recital and don't ever do it again unless you are prepared to confess yet again, etc., etc. For Father Connor, it was like administering a placebo to cure cancer.

But he supposed that their faith took them beyond the predictable nature of it all, and genuinely freed them from the burden of their most recent sins. At least he hoped it did. He only wished that he could find the same fulfillment.

It had been too long since he had experienced any of the dynamics that were supposed to accompany his calling. Most of his parishioners took it for granted that he was an enlightened man, that the Keys to the Kingdom were clutched in his certain grasp of the hereafter. They mistook his apathy for some sort of inner peace.

His dilemma was particularly acute when he was called upon to instruct prospective converts to the faith. A man, a woman, or a married couple would sit before him, eager to embark upon the journey to salvation. They would explain to him how they had come to this point in their lives, how they had been moved by something deep within themselves, or by some experience that they could not easily explain away. And he would nod and say, "Yes," and "yes." They would glean whatever they needed from that to confirm the rightness of their decisions, and would leave the old priest feeling more and more the useless icon.

He had prayed for deliverance from his weakness so many times that even the prayers had become numb and empty. He was running on pure habit.

But it hadn't always been so. He remembered clearly his youth, his early years as a firebrand in the Church. His acts, his works, and the passionate delivery of his sermons had earned him respect, and the grooming approval of the Roman hierarchy. It had all served to fulfill him in God. Evan Connor had been a stone-cold believer in his mission.

When he met the young Isaac Bloom, he was at the apex of his calling. And when Isaac had confessed his desire to convert, the priest had taken it as a personal tasking from On High. He had committed himself to the task with zeal. He had wanted to teach Isaac, to foster an appreciation for the wonder of the here and now while offering a glimpse beyond the celebration of the Mass to a mystical place where love eclipsed the weary burdens of the world.

In those first few months with Isaac, he too had come to believe in the possibility of all things. His mind and his spirit had expanded, and his daily partaking of the Host caused him to tremble with visions. At night, alone among the simple furnishings of his room, he would lay prone upon the floor and converse with God.

Then, a year after Isaac's emotional conversion, Evan Connor caught the attention of a controversial French priest who was doing some anthropological work in India: Pierre Chabot. Chabot had dedicated himself to the overlapping messages of love, compassion and tolerance in the world's oldest religions. Messages that he saw as a vital bond between all of humanity. Messages that might, one day, rid the world of the plague of war. He had heard of Evan, and had become fascinated by the almost heretical sermons that rang out like warning shots from Connor's pulpit.

For Connor had begun to question some of the Church's most fundamental paradigms. He saw a critical need for global birth control, particularly in the starving desperation of the Third World, where thousands of children each day were folding themselves into bony little balls of suffering and death.

Chabot knew something about the charges of heresy. He had been accused on more than one occasion of an over-zealous effort to undermine the teachings of Creationism. And his work in India's ancient places had taken on the trappings of exile. But above everything, he remained a devout man of God, who saw no threat to Heaven in the mysterious symbiosis of the world's oldest religions. Even when those religions were more worshipful of nature than cathedrals.

And he could see many of the same attitudes of loving rebellion in the young Irish priest here in London. It took a rare and unflinching courage to speak and act upon one's conscience, especially while adorned in the robes of the Holy Roman Empire.

Chabot could use such passionate commitment in his own search for truth.

Evan had been both flattered and frightened by Pierre's offer join his team. He prayed and contemplated the matter for a week. But, to Chabot's surprise, the young priest decided against it, and the Frenchman returned to India, where he would be excommunicated three years later. From that point on Evan Connor fell into the party line and abandoned his idealistic challenges to official doctrines.

It took the passage of many seasons for Connor to admit to himself that he had been afraid. To have gone off to work with Chabot would have placed him forever at odds with the political favorites of Rome. For the first time in his life, he had allowed his selfish interests to dominate his decisions. It was a habit he soon became comfortable with. And his once-powerful relationship with the Divine began to wither like a neglected flower.

A few months later, he accepted a safe and comfortable position in Boston. From there he would be able to see clearly to the rank of Cardinal. But the anticipated call had never come. And the once feared and dynamic Evan Connor had aged and grown weak in his own service.

Now, some fifty years after his first meeting with his one remaining friend, Father Connor was on the threshold of meeting his maker. The test results had been confirmed to him yesterday. Eight months to live, maybe less. And wasn't that a cosmic kick in the pants? He wondered if, after all this, he would ironically burn in Hell now that his faith was gone.

He stepped into the darkened interior of the confessional, looked back once more at the missed opportunities of his life, and sighed deeply. Then he slid back the screen and received the first of many, "Forgive me, Father, for I have sinned..."

—— * ——

Isaac finished up his article at home with six hours to spare on his deadline. The phone had rung every hour since his return, but his machine had fended off the anxious pleas of his editor until his work was complete. With the paying job accomplished, Isaac was free to concentrate solely upon the mystery that he had uncovered in Atlanta. He still could not guess at how long the murders had been taking place. His data only went back five years, but it seemed to him that the pattern was well in place even then.

For the next couple of weeks, he pored over his files and his notes, establishing the boundaries and the pattern to a point that would leave few questions as to its validity…at least in his own skeptical mind. As he did so, an uneasy awareness settled upon him. There would be another murder in Biloxi in approximately ten days.

Isaac began to tremble. It had been relatively easy to keep his emotional distance from this thing, to look at it as a sort of amateur detective game until now. But here was a black and white prediction of where and when another innocent life would be taken. This kind of knowledge had to be passed along to someone with resources and manpower. Someone who didn't have the uncomfortable feeling that it was more than mere coincidence that he had been in Atlanta that night. Someone who didn't feel trapped by the circumstances, and by the urgency of his own ghosts.

Like a reflex, he reached for the phone and dialed 911.

"Emergency services. How may we help you?"

Isaac stared at the receiver for several heart-pounding moments, then lowered it until it dangled from the end of his arm. The voice coming from the device asked questions regarding his health and safety. What could he tell her?

"A mass murderer will strike in Biloxi in less than two weeks, and I know this because I have done my homework. But I don't want you to think that I am involved...of course, I could be wrong about the whole thing...uh. Never mind."

Instead he spoke carefully into the mouthpiece, "I'm sorry, ma'am, I accidentally hit the wrong button on my memory dial."

He replaced the receiver and sat down to think about it for the hundredth time. He was boxed in. This "pattern" might well evaporate beneath the trained and analytical eyes of the authorities. Their obvious question would be, "Why does this seem so unusual to you?" That could be a difficult question to answer if Isaac came off as the only one interested in the matter. This would be followed by meaningful glances between the interrogators, with discreet notes taken in the margins of their official reports... "check personal info and question neighbors on the activities of one Isaac Bloom..."

Now a thought came that didn't even surprise him. It was if he had expected it on the heels of all the others. He had to go to Biloxi.

It was a long shot and would, probably, hopefully, involve a great deal of wasted time. But he would go, hole up in some comfortable hotel on the beach, and scan the obituaries every day until a likely prospect turned up. Morbid? Yes. But this would prove it or disprove it once and for all. And perhaps he could finally extract himself from this increasingly tangled web. Because the longer it dragged on, the more he felt himself a player and not a spectator.

He took a deep breath and leaned back in his chair, forcing the machinery of his mind into idle gear. He had been sitting very still, allowing his thoughts to flow unimpeded through his head, when the doorbell announced a visitor. He opened the front door to the weary frame of Evan Connor, standing there like a cardboard cutout. He invited him in.

"How are you, Evan?"

"Not bad, Isaac. I just thought I would stop by on my way back to the rectory. It is a lovely afternoon and I have been enjoying a walk. I haven't seen you in church in a while and I just wanted to make sure that you were all right. I've called a couple of times and gotten your machine, so I wasn't too concerned. I know that's how you dodge your pesky editors. But I thought I'd stop and say hello just the same."

The old priest had taken responsibility for Isaac's safety from the time he first arrived on the boat, following Evan from London to America. The habit had evolved over the years. And with the technological breakthrough of things like answering machines, they had devised a system where the old friends could check up with one another from their own homes. If Isaac was out of the house or away from the phone, or simply screening his calls, then the machine would pick up. If the answering machine did engage, Evan would call back with a three-ring query, at which time Isaac would pick up. The phone would never ring unanswered unless something was wrong. If Isaac was home and all right, and not dodging editors, then he would answer himself.

"Well, I'm glad you stopped by, Evan. I have just recently completed my latest assignment. It may well be my last. I think that it may be time to retire for good. Things are getting strange in this world of ours. In fact, there are a few matters I would like to discuss with you."

Evan looked carefully into Isaac's face. He could see fatigue. But there was something else there as well.

"I can appreciate your sentiments, Isaac. I have been feeling the call to leisure myself. I intend to speak with the Bishop next week about plans for my own retirement."

Isaac smiled. "That is news well-met. I have to say, I am surprised that you have waited this long. You have given so much to your flock. It's time that you enjoyed some time of your own beside those still waters."

The priest frowned and looked away. "Yes, I suppose that it is time to reflect some upon the winding road of my life. Maybe I'll go down to the Carolinas for some fishing..."

There was a wistful catch in his voice that invited Isaac to examine the gray sorrow of the priest's eyes. He realized with regret that he hadn't looked closely at his friend for many years. They had fallen into the routines of their private lives, both of them struggling under the burdens of their respective pasts, drifting along on the subtle currents of their losses.

Like so many in the church community, he had taken the priest for granted, knowing that he would always be there, ready to respond to any crisis promptly and with compassion. But where did priests go for their own renewal? Isaac sounded the depths in Evan's eyes. To his sad dismay, he saw that there was little fire there.

"What is bothering you, Evan?"

"I'm not quite sure," he replied stiffly. He hadn't decided how best to break the medical news to his friend. But he did feel a need to reveal his ennui, to pour the emptiness of his heart into the encouraging hands of his long-suffering comrade.

"There is a numbness that has overcome what I used to feel. Everything I do and say seems to echo with the hollow ring of doubt. I know that I am tired. But I think this may be more than retirement can cure. I am afraid to admit it," he paused and examined the edges of the rug beneath his feet, "but I feel that my faith has died."

Isaac took the priest by the arm and guided him over to a chair. He sat down across from him and tried to find a thread of thought upon which he could weave the meaning of the priest's life. But before he could say anything, Evan had risen and was looking down at Isaac with a worrying blankness in his eyes.

"I have become a phony. People come to me, to *me*," he emphasized by tapping himself on the chest, "for guidance and direction. But I am the most lost of the lost. And I have been for many years. The flock is following a shepherd who is astray in the wilderness. They are my responsibility. All of those souls seeking for God, and their priest hasn't been in touch with God for so long that God has moved away. I am so afraid. What has happened to me, Isaac?"

Isaac's mind was spinning and turning upon itself. Of all that seemed certain and solid in the upheaval of his world since his loss of Lessa, this priest had been the rock. Everything suddenly shifted beneath him, and the ground of his life fell away into the gravity of a foreign place.

His mind raced back to London. The circle had come back around. Evan Connor had once pulled him away from the brink of hopelessness and put him back in touch with some semblance of life. Now he sat here drowning in his own despair. Few things were worse than seeing an idealistic man shackled by the harsh jailers of disillusionment. The question was, what could he do for the priest when he, himself, so often struggled with a paltry faith?

"Evan, listen to me carefully. You have had a dramatic impact on countless lives, including my own. I have known you long enough to bear witness to that fact. What you are going through is common to the human experience. What would your faith really mean if it were never tested? You have often told me that suffering and uncertainty are necessary experiences for the forging of unshakeable faith. Take them into your own hands now, Father. This can only make you stronger."

Evan walked slowly to the window. The leaves had begun to betray the arrival of autumn. He considered the cycles of life. Perhaps he should have tried harder to recapture his friendship with God before old age had caught up to him. Now he could only look upon his coming death with a weary resignation. He was a priest who had come to doubt Heaven…to doubt the encompassing love that he had once implored Isaac to place his trust in.

“You are right, Isaac.” He spoke with his back to the room. “And I am tired. More than I have ever been. I will go back to the rectory to consider this some more. I’ll work my way through it.”

He turned and smiled at his friend as an offering of reassurance. As he started for the door, Isaac spoke quickly. Perhaps too quickly.

“Evan, why don’t you come to Biloxi with me? Take some time off. I’m not leaving for another five or six days. That will give you time to make some arrangements. We could play some golf, maybe spend a day at the track. What do you say?”

“Idiot!” Isaac’s mind barked at his spontaneous request. “What are you doing? You’re going to Biloxi to look for a serial killer! And you’re inviting a depressed priest to keep you company? Great idea. Why not take the entire catechism class as well… make it a field trip…”

But the weary priest solved his dilemma. “No, thanks. I wouldn’t be good company, though I do thank you for the offer. Something tells me that I need to spend more time alone with this. But I’ll see you at Mass before you leave.”

He stepped across the threshold of the door, leaving Isaac relieved, concerned, and more than a little anxious.

He had almost confessed to Evan the mess that he was in. But Evan’s problems precluded that. And if he couldn’t confess it to the priest, at least for now, then he couldn’t share it with anyone.

CHAPTER SIX

Five days later he was sprawled beside a pool on the Biloxi strand, sipping a Cotes de Provence. The bone-dry Rose had a mineral crispness that was the perfect antidote to the humid afternoon. Aside from the habit of enjoying an expensive wine, he was involved in his other habit...waiting. He was trying to absorb a Kesey novel, but the fluid prose kept catching in the rocky shallows of his preoccupation. A stranger was about to die. He or she might be out on the streets right now, looking for a handout, a kindness from some unconcerned passerby. But, if his theories were correct, that person would be dead within a week, and would no longer depend upon the used-up compassion of a used-up world.

He daubed sunscreen on his flaking nose. He was trying to accept the last true warmth of the season even as he was trying to accept his purpose here. The spectrum of emotions wrapped up in this matter utterly fatigued him. This was no place for a grieving, past-dwelling old man to be. And he consciously knew it. His days should be spent in the writing of memoirs and the tender handling of faded photographs. That was all he wanted, and nothing more. To draw the shades and lean back in a chair... and think of her in terms of there, and there. To wait, to wait...for that hopeful evening, that last lonely night when he would finally close his eyes and there would be no more dreams…there would be only Lessa, always.

But for now he *was* here. Reading the papers twice a day, anticipating a death that was perhaps even now moving among its potential victims.

He found himself drinking too much as he waited. This had always been a lurking problem. For fifty years he had kept a wary eye on that jinni. Now, with time to kill—time waiting for the kill—he was turning more and more to the liquid easings of a troubled conscience.

Perhaps the most unsettling aspect of his involvement with these murders was the fact that his nocturnal imagining were becoming increasingly vivid and disturbing. Memories he had thought mostly buried were suddenly lumbering like zombies among the landscapes of his dreams: the camp, the cries, the foot-dragging shuffle of the oven-feeders. He hadn't slept well since Atlanta. "Hell," he thought sourly, "I haven't slept well since my wedding night."

He shaded his eyes and looked obliquely at the sun to judge the time. He never wore a watch. Time had never been his friend, so why remind himself of its cruel passage? It looked to be about two. He would waste another hour and then go in for a shower and a brief nap. The sun and the wine were draining his resolve, and he had probably spent too much time in the company of both already.

He closed his eyes behind his sunglasses, felt the muscled tension of his fatigue and tried to pinpoint it but couldn't. Instead of fighting, he let it take him completely. As he succumbed to a restless slumber, he heard a child crying out on the strand. "Mommy, mommy!…"

"…Mommy, mommy!..." The child, a boy of eight or nine years, darted past them, weaving his way through the throng of strangers, seeking the comfort of his family. On the breast pocket of his black coat was sewn the yellow Star of David: the identifier of their race. Isaac watched the boy as he ran through that sea of yellow stars…as some children, somewhere far from Warsaw, might be running through a field of sunflowers.

All around them, the dense mass plodded forward, pulling carts and dragging trunks and luggage as if they were about to board the Titanic. All the mementos of a doomed people, already dead, but not yet buried…not yet burned.

The members of their once proudly-defiant clique had dressed in black, as in mourning, and had set out for the ghetto, as ordered by the Nazis. The entire Jewish population was being relocated so that the Germans could "ensure their safety from a hostile population." Patrik had insisted that they link arms and sing Jewish folk songs. "A solidarity of the damned," he had icily remarked. They had posed for a final photograph as free Polish youth before they were herded into the walled death-pool of the ghetto.

Isaac was amazed at the resolve and the repose of his friends. In particular, Lessa seemed almost a stranger when compared to her previously-fearful self. His wife was now a leader among the young Jews. Her humor and compassion were sought out by all who knew her.

By contrast, Isaac was almost numb with apprehension. There had been rumors of this day for many weeks. Now they were passing away from their old lives and entering a time and place where they were at the mercy of a machine that wanted only their removal.

He could only imagine the worst. A great many of their people had already been shipped away from Warsaw. No one knew for certain where these people had gone, but there were horrible rumors of mass killings, and open graves where hundreds upon hundreds had gone to their end. When he pondered these things—it was impossible for him not to—when he thought of his beloved Lessa at the hands of these butchers, he would nearly go mad with anxiety.

For the next five months, Isaac waited breathlessly for the knock at their door. Each morning would find yet another family gone, taken from their community. The terror was brilliant in its execution: a three a.m. pounding at the door, the jackboot rush through the rooms, the bellowed threats and blows as they were rounded up and shoved onto waiting trucks already loaded with the startled, sobbing faces of the lost.

Isaac knew that terror. He was the prime example of what terror was meant to inflict. A paralyzed waiting…a seasickness of certain disaster. The Nazis didn't even need to come for people like Isaac. He was already a psychological slave to their will. Their random calculations, their night-terror tactics, had done the lion's share of their work. Auschwitz was merely a formality.

But Isaac was no coward. His fear was not for himself. The way his mind left him was a dark fantasy, an opportunity for the escape he had denied his wife. The moment had played itself out before him in so many ways and with so many happy endings that, after a month or two of waiting for them to come for Lessa and himself, he came to prefer the only place where they were safe…the sanctuary of his escapist thoughts.

Lessa knew what was happening to her husband. But she had chosen to immerse herself in a routine of mercy and service. There were many lost souls in the ghetto. Food was scarce. There were few medicines to help the sick. Lessa did what she could with her creative compassion. And each day she would attempt to enlist the aid of the man she loved and still believed in.

But Isaac stayed off the streets and implored her to do the same. The illusion of locked doors was a comfort to him. There, he could wrap a blanket about his shoulders and devise clever methods of escape. His schemes grew more fantastic and bizarre with each passing day. He would fill blank pages with the details of complex plans dependent upon split-second timing and bold daring. Then, as he ran headlong through the thickets of his imagination, he would come to a clearing and see the folly of it all, and sink once more into a shuddering despair. "Oh, Lessa!" he would cry out in his anguish. "What have I done to you?"

Lessa prayed for his recovery. But she would not join him in his hopelessness. She was unmoved by the weapons and the swagger of the Nazis. She could guess easily enough at their motives. She was not ignorant to their intentions for her people. But she knew that much of their power came from the easy surrender that they depended upon. She could withhold that from them, if nothing else. And if she were meant to die then she would die in a place that their terror couldn't reach.

So Isaac withered as she blossomed; she renounced her fear for all time, proclaiming her faith in love above all else. She swore that she would make him see. Somehow, someday, she would find the keys to unlock Isaac's courageous, powerful love. This was her sacred promise to both of them. It was her prayer to God on the very night they came for Isaac and Lessa Bloom.

Isaac awakened with a sudden astonishment of sorrow and stared blankly at the shimmering surface of the pool. He shook the lingering cobwebs from his head. What he wouldn't give for some real rest, some dreamless sleep. Maybe another bottle of wine would grant his wish. He peeled himself off the lounger and walked stiffly to his room.

CHAPTER SEVEN

Three days later he was completely bored and bewildered. There hadn't been anything in the Biloxi obituaries that would even qualify as being remotely similar. He had been so certain that the pattern was going to be perpetuated here. But now he was having third and fourth thoughts about the entire affair.

He made up his mind to give it three more days, then fly back to Boston and forget the entire morbid business. In the meantime, a new thought occurred to him. One born of too much monotony and perhaps a little too much juice of the vine—but he decided to become less of a passive observer. He intended to find a likely locale and make a few rounds. Maybe he could learn something about the motives or methods behind the killings just by being out there among those people. Maybe he could see what the killer was seeing…tap into his thoughts.

He spent the next afternoon shopping for menswear of the second-hand variety. He purchased a natty pair of wool trousers, a polo-type shirt with a fetching jungle-cat motif above the breast pocket, a light jacket with a busted zipper, and a rather extravagant silver-knobbed walking stick. The latter was a surprise find, but a comforting one. He offered his platinum card for payment, but the young, bepimpled clerk only yawned at him.

"We ain't set up to handle credit cards. All five locations of the Scrimp-a-Lot chain deal only in cash."

"Ah. Of course. Sorry. Here you are, then. Twenty-four fifty. And would you mind hailing me a taxi, please?"

"There's a phone down by the QuikeeMart. Have a nice day."

Back at his hotel, Isaac waited until the darkness had settled completely over the Gulf shores, then called a taxi from his room. He told the driver to take him to "where the homeless people spend their nights." The driver answered him with a very disapproving expression but shrugged his shoulders and pulled away from the curb.

He deposited Isaac at a poorly-lit intersection and pointed across the street to the darkened interior of Evangeline Park. As the cab sped off, Isaac suppressed the nagging fear and knee-jerk reminders of his night in Atlanta. He was somewhat comforted by the fact that he had promised the driver a twenty-dollar tip to return in ninety minutes, and had gotten an eager affirmative.

He walked into the park and paused, allowing his eyes time to adjust to the lesser light. Then, like apparitions divorcing themselves from the backdrop of the night, he saw them in their numbers. The American refugees. Even more than he had seen in Atlanta.

Most of them were already lying down for the night. There were small groups of men smoking and talking among the reclining figures on the ground and the low benches. He walked deeper into the park's darkness.

After fifteen minutes of aimless wandering, ignored by the few night-walkers that he passed, he came to the silent, shadowed heart of Evangeline Park. He concealed himself in a small stand of trees, where his instincts told him to stay put for a while. There didn't seem to be anything more that he could do.

He pulled a travel flask from the breast pocket of his jacket and sipped at the expensive brandy, reassured by its familiar warmth.

Isaac, ever the observer of life's ironies and strange circumstances, shook his head at the fact that here he was, dressed in a manner to suggest he belonged at this calloused juncture of time and space, sipping 25-year-old brandy that cost as much as any one of these people were likely to see in months of begging. Their lives could hardly be more different, on the surface of things. Yet... there were certain shared experiences. He could relate to them on certain levels. And just by pausing among them...just by passing through...he could feel the palpable anxiety that never rested, that slept with one eye forever open. Perhaps this was why he kept allowing himself to be pulled more deeply into the mystery of their demise.

Half an hour passed. Forty-five minutes. An hour. He shifted, then began to pace in a tight circle under the cover of the trees. The brandy was long-since drained and he would have to be heading back to the street soon.

Then, faintly, he heard it. A stifled cry had somehow found its way to his ears. He stopped breathing and strained his will to listen. He could hear his own heart pounding like a hammer on an anvil, and he was certain that it would drown out any other sound that might straggle through these trees. But there! He heard it again. A low moaning, certainly one of distress. He moved quickly but quietly in the direction of the sound, picking his way through the trees, avoiding the exposed roots and fallen branches in his path.

Then again, fainter but somehow closer. Just ahead he could make out a bench and two figures, one bent over another splayed recklessly across it. He was mesmerized by the scene, and before he was aware of it he had approached to within six feet.

Something was quite wrong. There was a weak, whimpering cry, almost drowned out by another, more disturbing noise. Greedy, hungry, almost lewd. Sucking. He was beyond compelled and, without a second thought, hit the switch on the flashlight.

He was nearly knocked back by what he saw bathed in the sudden light.

The kneeling figure turned swiftly and rose towards him. Isaac caught a brief moment of madness in the light's beam. A tube dangled from the arm of the man on the bench, blood spurting from it like the damaged water fountain he had passed earlier. The face of the man who came at him was smeared with it, dark and wet and obscene, before the light was knocked savagely from his trembling hand.

Then the stranger had him by the throat, his face close to Isaac's own. There was no bottom to the well-dark eyes that looked into his. He was squeezing the very life from Isaac's lungs when the situation changed abruptly. The man loosened his grip and stared harder into Isaac's wide eyes.

"I know you," he whispered. "Where have we met, old man?"

Isaac took the opportunity to thrust his cane up between them, bringing the silver-knobbed handle into a violent collision with the man's chin, and sending him staggering just long enough for Isaac to turn and flee.

He had covered less than a hundred feet when he ran straight into the arms of another man, coming up the narrow path with four others. The sudden encounter took them all by surprise. Isaac stifled a yell, realized that this was an inadvertent rescue, and composed himself quickly. He looked back over his shoulder as five questioning voices rushed at him. He turned back to them and hastily explained that he had just witnessed an assault. They all hurried back to the scene, but there was no sign of what Isaac had described. Nothing at all. Even his flashlight had vanished.

Now the men turned their eyes on him. Someone muttered something about the smell of serious alcohol on Isaac's breath and another ventured a question as to whether he had a pass from the shelter to be out so late. Then they walked deliberately away from him. And Isaac walked quickly back out of the park, to practically leap into his waiting taxi.

Back in his room, Isaac could not stop trembling. He turned on every light in the entire suite and drank steadily from the bottle of Remy on the credenza.

"It was insanity! That man was drinking the other man's blood! No, Isaac, no. There is no way that that was what you saw," he reassured himself weakly.

He dropped to his knees, Cognac in hand, and prayed with fervor. Then he crawled into bed, intellectually and emotionally spent, as the macabre scene replayed itself over and over before his clamped eyes. Right on cue, visions of Auschwitz joined in the conspiracy to unravel the edges of his remaining mind. The flames and the smoke of the ovens, the horrific cries. He thought the he had left the core of that smoldering nightmare behind him. It was the 1990's now. But what he had just witnessed was more like nineteenth-century fiction.

Some sick creature was drinking the blood of vagrants. He obviously had delusions that Bram Stoker could understand. And he was preying on those who were less likely to struggle with any sort of vigor. Because he had no fangs, he was using some sort of syringe and tube contraption and slurping away like a fuel thief siphons from an unwatched car.

Isaac knew that there was a wayward group of misfits in New Orleans who wore eye liner and pierced their bodies in unimaginable places. They dressed in costume every waking day and wandered the city by night. They desperately assured everyone who would listen that they were vampires. But the person he saw on this night was taking their childish fantasies to a whole new level.

Was he responsible for the morphine as well? And how could he know that his victims were already dying? That went way beyond the credibility of coincidence. Was he a doctor? What doctor would have access to that many medical histories? Hell, those kinds of people didn't even have medical histories.

Wait. Maybe that wasn't the killer he was after. Maybe that was some other wacko who happened to be out tonight. Yes. That must be it. "But why did he think he knew me?" Isaac asked himself miserably. Oh lord. What was he going to do?

Calling the police seemed more impossible than ever. There was no body. No evidence. And the men that he had encountered after the fact, if they could be identified and questioned at all, would only relate the story of a babbling old boozer stumbling around after phantoms in the dark.

His thoughts blurred into a frantic helplessness until he finally succumbed to another restless sleep.

By noon the next day he felt only slightly better. The knot of anxiety in his gut refused to loosen. This was due to the fact that he had decided to take one more step in this gruesome dance.

His research had been proven valid. The next murder would take place in St. Louis. He would go there and wait again. But this time he would be more careful, and in no way confront the situation. If the killer hadn't been scared off, Isaac intended to somehow entice a witness to the scene and let that person be the one to inform the authorities.

It was absurd, he knew. But by now none of it could claim the realm of sanity. And deep down he had to confess to something more than a passing interest. His subconscious had made some sort of connection between the horror this man was wreaking upon the homeless and the horror his wife had suffered at the brutal hands of the Nazis.

He was very involved with this thing now, and he would have to see it through to the end. That incessant question kept echoing in his head, "Where have we met, old man?" How could he possibly have remembered Isaac from Atlanta? It was so dark that they hadn't even gotten a good look at each other…

CHAPTER EIGHT

He could not have said how he knew it, but as his plane cruised towards St. Louis, he was aware that a turning point was at hand. Something was going to happen there that would bring this matter out into the light.

When he arrived, he gathered the information he would need to become a vagrant for the night. There was an old warehouse section along the river that the city's homeless called home. The abandoned buildings offered shelter from the inclement weather. And the police were a little more tolerant of them if they kept to this part of town. This is where Isaac would go.

He contemplated buying a gun. But the very notion only served to remind him of how far in over his head he already was. The idea that he would be able to, first, discern the true threat from the host of homeless wanderers, and then to muster the intellectual commitment necessary to take someone out of this world for good…not to mention the terrible responsibility of becoming someone else's judge, jury and executioner? No. He was trying very hard to keep everything in some sort of workable perspective. Introducing a loaded weapon into the proceedings would tilt the mindset dramatically, from objectivity to an almost passive-aggressive state in which everyone he would encounter would be an existential threat.

In his rationale, this was a kind of experiment, really…another project for a future article. It was still just beyond his comprehension that there was a blood-drinking killer stalking these southern cities…and one who seemed to know him. No, no. Keep the mind balanced. Let it deal with things familiar, focus on the ordinary aspects of it all. Just a little research, a little homework, a little silver crucifix in the trouser pocket, just in case…

He spent the next four days in his hotel room, reading, drinking good wine, and preparing himself as best he could psychologically. More than a little prayer, and Mass on Sunday. Monday night found him dressed in his third-hand attire, standing on another dimly lit and littered street outside a warehouse that could not remember the last days of its usefulness. His taxi roared off with instructions to return in two hours.

He wandered through several vast, high-ceilinged rooms, cathedral-like in the sooty darkness. His flashlight was clutched in his hand, but his eyes had adjusted and he wouldn't use it unless circumstances dictated. It was nearly ten p.m., and many of the people he had seen were reclined or sleeping. But these buildings were so big, and spread out over such an area, that he felt entirely alone.

There wasn't any plan to his movements. How could there be? Instead, he allowed his instincts to guide him once again. They had proven themselves in Biloxi. And maybe in Atlanta? There was another in a line of eerie thoughts. Had he somehow been drawn to Piedmont Park that night?

Had Lessa whispered into his subconscious that he should uncharacteristically leave the luxury of his hotel suite and take a random nocturnal stroll among Atlanta's economic refugees? The thought was enough to make his head spin, but it was certainly a valid idea in light of everything that had occurred since. And he was incapable of abandoning it. This was all beginning to feel a little too predestined.

After nearly two hours of wandering and waiting, he gave up and returned to his hotel.

He repeated the scenario for the next three nights. Some of the locals had begun to regard him suspiciously. But in the end he was just another old man with insomnia. Restless with wasted time. Most of them could identify with that.

On the fourth night, he poked among the empty buildings on the easternmost edge of the warehouse complex. He had come to a point of ending and peered into the inky depths of an old river shed. He was even more anxious than usual. But each time he had started to leave, something equally anxious had stopped him from doing so.

He held a mental conversation with Lessa, attempting to bolster his fading resolve. For some reason, Lessa's side of the conversation encouraged him to pursue this, and he wondered aloud why that would be the case. Why on Earth would he assume her position to be that one? Why wouldn't she usher him hastily back to the comfort of his Boston home? He could almost hear her soft, certain words.

"There is no 'safety,' Isaac. Life is the most dangerous thing one can participate in. But you must trust in something beyond yourself if you would be free. And that 'something' is the greatest power in the universe. Love, my darling. Love..."

Isaac was deeply absorbed in this line of thought when a finger tapped him lightly on the shoulder. He whirled and hit the light switch in one motion. The beam probed at the vacant darkness. He whirled again, stabbing with the light, willing it to discover the source of his sudden terror. A phantom voice ran up the notches of his spine..."You are looking in the wrong place."

Now he turned again, this time with an infinite slowness, back to the building's interior. He was there, right in front of him. "Oh, God," Isaac gasped audibly. The man's lips were curled in a kind of smile, but his eyes were stone.

Before Isaac could draw another breath, the stranger placed the long nail of his right index finger onto the back of his own tongue and drew it sharply forward, leaving a crimson wake. Without pausing, he grabbed Isaac by the left wrist and inserted his bloody nail into the vein on the back of Isaac's hand. There was no pain. There was, however, a sensation of luxurious surrender. Decades of worry and desire vanished like a sigh on the wind.

The man reached into Isaac's breast pocket and removed his wallet, glancing quickly at the driver's license. "There isn't enough light," Isaac thought. "I can barely see his face..." But the man spoke calmly and in perfect control.

"Hear me well, Isaac Bloom. From this moment forward, you are mine. Your very thoughts will be revealed to me if I should inquire of them. You will obey me completely and without question. I tell you these things for your own information because in all other respects you will function as usual. I will determine your fate, but it won't be tonight. There are too many questions to consider. Arrangements will be made for you to fly to New Orleans on tomorrow's afternoon flight. When you arrive, you will check in to the Crescent Esplanade Hotel. At ten p.m. you will go, on foot, to the Blue Note bar on Conti St., and you will wait for me there. Now, go and find the taxi that has awaited you these past four nights, and return to your hotel."

Isaac stood and watched the man disappear back into the shadows. He walked the five blocks to his rendezvous point and waited for his ride. When the cab pulled to the curb, the driver turned and studied the old man closely.

"If you don't mind my asking, mister, what have you been doing out there for the last couple of hours?"

"Just a little research project on the homeless." Isaac brushed the question aside, already aware of his inability to mention the stranger in any manner.

"Well, Pops, I don't know if this is a compliment or an insult, but you sure are dressed for the part. You're natural. Hey! Did you know that you're bleeding?"

Isaac peered down at his hand for the first time. The blood had now clotted, but had left a dried trail that passed beneath his wedding band and ended at the tip of his finger.

"It's just a scratch," he responded automatically. "The hotel, please."

Back in his room, Isaac sat upright on the edge of the bed. His thoughts were entirely lucid. But, try as he might, he could not will himself to ask for help. At one point he had reached for the phone to call the police. As soon as he started to speak, however, he could hear his blood, his essence, singing out against it. It was the oddest sensation, to be able to think rationally, to know what needed to be done. But when he tried to rouse himself to action, he lost all concern. He was not afraid. For the first time in as long as he could remember, he was not afraid. But he was well aware that he was in grave danger.

At four o'clock the next day he boarded the plane for a return trip to New Orleans.

CHAPTER NINE

Isaac checked into the hotel as commanded. Definitely off the Quarter's beaten path, it was a common affair that would have been given two very reluctant stars in Europe. He carried his own luggage up three flights of stairs. Roaches scurried for cover when he opened the door, but there wasn't much. A stained and threadbare rug, two risky chairs bristling with springs, and a bed that sagged so badly he could have bathed in the middle of it. These were his forlorn welcome to his new (and final?) home. He had asked the desk man what his arrangements were, and how long he was paid up for. He was given a curious expression and a mumbled message that, if deciphered, would have been, "You pay by the night, fool."

At nine-fifteen he showered, dressed casually, and headed out for the Blue Note. Upon his arrival, he found that he was capable of ordering a brandy, and almost anything else that didn't threaten his new-found acquaintance. Then he sat back to wait.

The bar was poorly attended. There was no music, even though the jukebox near his table screamed with neon-promises of three for a dollar. A few strains of Bourbon Street jazz would occasionally poke their heads in out of curiosity, but quickly departed, leaving a monotonous silence.

He had consumed half a tumbler of brandy when he began to notice something else unusual about his thoughts. His recollections, to be precise, were much more vivid and detailed than they had been even recently. There was a sharp sense of "nowness" to them. He had been thinking of Lessa almost exclusively since arriving. It had been like stepping into the past.

He didn't know when the stranger would arrive. But he felt compelled to test this phenomenon of fresh-memory even further. He closed his eyes and conjured his most poignant moment with his wife. He could feel it rushing towards him…just as he had then. He could hear the steel rails singing the dirge of the death car beneath them. The long, mournful whistle, passing sadly from box to box, from heart to breaking heart. This was the ride to Auschwitz. These were his last hours with Lessa.

The Nazis had rounded them up in the very early hours, allowing them one suitcase of their most valued possessions. Lessa insisted on leaving everything behind. "Let's travel light," she had smiled and squeezed his hand even as they were shoved onto the trucks.

It was another "relocation." A safer place where they could work and live in peace until the tensions had subsided. A pleasant camp in the country. Everyone, by now, had heard the gamut of dark rumors. But, as there was no choice in boarding the trains, many chose to cling to the lies rather than slip from the secure arms of sanity. There would be time for madness later.

Except for Isaac. He was embracing his madness now. With each passing moment, with each foot of the rails that the train devoured, he slipped farther away from his wife.

She held him in the darkness, trying to absorb his anguish. But the wailing and the tears around them were no comfort to the comfortless. Lessa pulled him into a crowded corner and pleaded with him to be strong.

"Dear God, Isaac. Please speak to me. Please, hold me."

But his eyes were vacant. He had pulled the plug on his thoughts and feelings. It was his only defense from what was happening right now. They sank to the floor together, and the train rocked them like children in a cradle. Isaac broke down and wept into the folds of her dress as remorse gnawed hungrily at his heart.

Lessa spoke again, urgency in her soft voice.

"Isaac, there is something I've been meaning to tell you. Do you remember that day in the field, right after we were married, when we made love in the rain? And do you remember how we talked about one day going to the Greek Islands, how we would look at the beautiful pictures and drink Ouzo on the floor of your mother's house? Well, darling, that day in the field, when you were inside of me…I went there. It was so lovely, Isaac, better than the pictures. The breeze was warm, and we walked in the sand, and we made love in the sea. Oh Isaac, I want us to go there now! You and me, far away from here. The others in this car won't notice. Let us touch each other. Let us love each other…"

Isaac raised his head slowly and looked into her pleading eyes. She amazed him. It was all there. She was still his wife, after all. He had drifted out upon the frightful currents of the midnight sea, but she was still tending the shore-fires for him, and was calling him back to her now. She asked him to go with her once before, and he had refused. He would not refuse her again.

They rose together and pressed back into the corner. The sway of the car gave discretion to their movements. Their mouths opened to one another and his hands moved over her, feeling the slow curves of her breasts, the purifying fire between her legs, and she consumed him with it. Burning away the pain, the sorrow, leaving only white ashes in the embers of her forgiveness. He felt it now. The power coursed through their connected bodies like a thick chord. They were there, and they were laughing, swinging in a hammock, sharing a cool drink as the island music eclipsed the rail song. Then they were running in the sand, shedding their clothes like those two innocent children that they had always been. It was the sea. It was the sky. It was all. They arched against the current and they gasped against the sky. The seabirds cried out above them, and cried out again. And then, the long doppler of the whistle as the train slowed into the village of Birkenau.

"Juden, raus! Raus!"

The blinding lights of the Auschwitz platform drove like spikes into their car and pried the fearful from their huddled corners, drawing them all forward onto the dock. Under such nightmarish conditions one expected a madness, a chaos of confusion. But there was no confusion. The madness would not be tolerated... only allowed, when the Nazis allowed it. And they would allow it. The fabled German efficiency was very much in evidence.

Two lines were formed. Two impersonal, forever-goodbye lines that somehow managed to progress as though a vital thing were happening...as though the business at hand was were quite necessary to some cosmic purpose. It was simple and thorough and without the slightest ceremony, this vocation, this commerce, this genocide.

Lessa clung to Isaac's hand until the last possible moment, when it was savagely wrenched from her by a guard. Isaac was shoved up ahead of her into a separate line, too numb to speak, to cry out. He turned and looked back at her, and a lifetime of conversation passed through the pleas of a people, through the tearful implorings of the panicking crowd, and rang like church bells in their breaking hearts.

Lessa had held her tears for as long as she could, and now they fell freely upon her face. But her gaze remained fixed on her husband, strong and constant. His hands were shaking so badly that he was certain she could see them, and he thrust them into his pockets as he was pressed forward. It was a machine, Isaac suddenly realized. It was a machine with gears and levers and a terrible purpose. And his people were the grist.

For a moment, shock overcame him and he found himself staring down at the concrete beneath his feet, wondering at the untold tears that had fallen there. This was beyond Hell, beyond the reaches of mercy. Nothing could save them. Nothing could even offer the slimmest hope of salvation. This was the boundary of midnight.

As the darkness descended upon him, he looked back once more, straining over the oceanic grief, and caught a final moment of her. She stretched her arms out toward him, and her words flew into his black surrender.

"Believe, Isaac! I believe in forever! This place has no power over love! I love you, Isaac, I love..."

She was slapped harder than he had ever seen anyone hit in his life, and knocked to the ground. He moved in a blur and got to within five feet of the man who had suddenly taught him the meaning of hate when he was struck in the side of the head with the butt of a rifle. And as the darkness rose up to claim him, as the long, solitary night of his life was born there on the tear-washed concrete of Auschwitz, he knew that he was seeing his wife for the last time.

Isaac shook his head from side to side, still reeling from the blow. The recollection was so powerful that his skull felt shattered. He touched it, expecting to feel the flow of blood and the tapestry of torn skin. There were tears on his face. The murderer was seated across from him.

The two of them sat there in silence as the minutes fell away. Isaac wiped at his eyes, wanting to face the killer with dignity. There was an instant transference of rage from the Nazi who had slapped Lessa to the man who sat now before him.

A waitress appeared at their table and the stranger ordered brandy, Isaac's poison. He looked the man over carefully. One certainly could not judge the book from the cover. This was a well-groomed cat, one that was accustomed to the finer things. Just slightly gray, just slightly exotic, he was dressed for a European train, or a Jules Verne balloon, all linen and worsted wool. The watch was expensive, but not commercial. The look on the man's face was one of vague amusement…and this stoked the fire of Isaac's rage.

"I am Julian Germain. And I am quite curious, Mr. Bloom, to know where we have met." He spoke the words as statement of fact and curious condescension at once. Isaac's response issued forth like a spring flood.

"It was in Atlanta…Piedmont Park…last month. The night you killed the old woman with the doll." Isaac gazed into the chalkboard blackness of Julian's eyes. "Why was that necessary?"

Julian seemed mildly surprised by the answer, and the ensuing question.

"First of all," he replied, "you will notice that your thoughts are your own, but that at my bidding you will reveal them to me. Therefore you may only ask questions until I tire of them. Or of you. Secondly, you very nearly perished that night. You are most fortunate to have survived to this point. One might say that you are blessed. As I watched you wandering the warehouses in St. Louis, I knew that you were seeking me…or something like me. I do recall you now.

"You were out of your element. There are no "visitors" of your age in that park after the sun has departed. At first I mistook you for one of them…one of the walking dead. But when you paused there on the path I sensed an odd contradiction. There is death in you, but there is something else…something. In any case, I haven't killed anyone with the true life-light in a very long while. So I passed you by. But I would like to know why you were there. And more importantly, how you came to find me in Biloxi and St. Louis."

Isaac explained how he had experienced a sort of bonding with the old woman, and that after reading of her death in the obituaries, he had connected it with their encounter on the path.

"It was really just a strange series of coincidences that led me to you. Call it dumb, and very bad, luck."

"Hm," Julian looked unimpressed. "I hardly believe in coincidence. Tell me then, what were you thinking about when I arrived? Was it the fear of dying that brought tears to your eyes?"

Isaac shifted in his seat. He had no desire to divulge the details of his personal pain. But it was out of his hands.

"I was thinking of the last time I saw my wife."

Julian could see that the response had been wrenched from him. He could sense a strength that he would not have guessed at in the dark warehouse in St. Louis. He wondered where it came from.

"And when, and where, was that?" He asked without emotion.

"1943. Auschwitz."

The stranger responded with the slightest wincing of the eyes. He reached across the table and took Isaac's wrist, turned it over and gazed at the tattoo. Then he turned to the bar and motioned with a raised hand.

Moments later, a very old bottle of Cognac arrived. Julian poured generously into Isaac's glass, then two fingers into his own. He stared at Isaac with a precise observation.

"The Cognac is pre-phylloxera, very old. There is precious little of it left in this world. As the vines of Europe were being laid to waste by the grape-plague, it took the grafting of American vines (which, ironically, had caused the issue in the first place) to salvage the vineyards of the Old World. But we shall miss this old Cognac when it is gone." He raised his glass to Isaac's. "So let us enjoy the past. It becomes more precious with the disappointments of time."

Isaac raised the amber fluid to his nose and inhaled deeply. Oh yes. This was a rare treasure. And there was that odd sensation again. He could appreciate the artistry and the significance of the wine and want to linger over it. There was a certain implication there, but it flitted away from him. Julian wasn't finished singing its praises.

"This brandy is older than you. Taken with loving care from the nurturing womb of the barrel and allowed to spill like a dreamy jinni into the bottle. As that transference was taking place, hundreds and thousands of young men from dozens of countries were crawling forward on their muddied bellies. Crawling wormlike over the decomposing bodies of their comrades, under the razor wire, around the mines, through the ooze and the slime and the rotting death of the First World War. The newspapers referred to it as 'Trench Warfare.' The soldiers referred to it as Hell." With that, Julian took a mouthful of the amber liquid, inhaled over it, swallowed and exhaled slowly as Isaac's brow furrowed in pain. "This century has been even more brutal than all before it. As man evolves technologically, to the point where *all* life now lives in the shadow of an existential threat, he regresses in his humanity. I have witnessed that regression for some six hundred years."

He arched his eyebrows and watched Isaac's response with that same vague smile. Isaac swallowed hard. This man was obviously quite insane. But at the instant the thought entered his mind, it was swept effortlessly aside by a profound sense of the truth. Julian drank blood because he was a vampire.

Julian's eyes remained on Isaac's face as he continued to add to the surrealism of the moment.

"There is a great deal of sorrow within you. That is the death I sensed that night. But it is balanced by something I haven't quite identified..."

Isaac suddenly interrupted him with the question that he had been carrying for weeks.

"How could you have known that all of your victims were dying?"

"Your two questions are connected, Mr. Bloom. You asked why it was necessary to kill the old woman. And you wonder how I knew that they were dying. Finish your drink. There are things to discuss while the night is yet innocent of answers. We will walk for awhile."

Isaac drained his glass, keenly aware of the differences in the two brandies he had consumed this night. He had only had Cognac that good on one other occasion. It seemed a shame to drain his glass so abruptly.

As they exited the bar, Isaac was amazed at how relaxed he felt. How matter-of-fact it all seemed. There was such an absence of concern that it almost left him giddy.

They neared the heart of the Quarter and the music and revelry paraded around them. They were among the full strength of the tourists now. Isaac was wondering at their destination when Julian broke the spell.

"Look around you, Isaac, and pick a club or a bar at random. There is something I want you to see."

Isaac stopped and turned 360 degrees in the street. On the opposite corner was an establishment with what seemed an appropriate name: The Zoo.

"Whatever you have in mind, I'm confident that we can find it there."

Julian frowned and led the way into the club.

CHAPTER TEN

"The Zoo," indeed. As they entered, Isaac felt almost foolish for choosing such a dive. The place was deserted except for three rather unwholesome characters, who lounged contemptuously at a littered table near the wall. But The Zoo was a two-story affair. And what was down in no way prepared Isaac for what was up.

There was muted, high-decibel music coming from above them. In looking for it, Isaac found a dark hallway that kept the staircase a secret. Julian was already there. He glanced once at Isaac and began his ascent. The stairs ended at a heavy steel door with a sliding screen that would not have been out of place in an old gangster movie. Julian rang the bell, and after several minutes the screen slid back and a pair of thickly-browed eyes peered out at them.

The door swung open and Isaac was assaulted by music, incense, and the chaos of lasers. Unimagined spectrums of light careened off the walls and mirrors. The floor itself was a kaleidoscope of color. Alice had tumbled into the looking glass.

It was one vast room. The furnishings were limited to cushions and futon mattresses thrown randomly about. Two of the four corners offered cocktails. Isaac noticed that the art on the walls was of a specifically voluptuous nature. The incense was doing a poor job of masking the unmistakable aroma of premium marijuana.

Through this carelessly-hedonistic landscape was a hungry wandering of men and women of all ages and all social backgrounds. This was a meeting place of the sensually-jaded...the envelope-pushers who had stepped beyond the boundaries of "normal" eroticism too often, and who could no longer be satisfied by less esoteric pleasures.

In the middle of the room they were dancing. At least, Isaac supposed that dancing was the proper coinage. But two was not the common pairing. More often it was three or four people together. They moved against one another with a kind of serpentine friction. The jarring acoustics served to mute the private jargon of their public voracity.

Isaac looked at Julian as if to ask, "What is this all about?" Julian was taking it all in with a serious intent that seemed out of place. He surveyed the scene with a scrutiny that Isaac felt fortunate not to be the object of.

Julian's gaze had come to rest upon a small group of men reclining on one of the futons not far from where they stood. They surrounded a willowy, sandy-haired young woman of considerable beauty. The men took turns touching her and speaking into her ear. She seemed hardly to notice. Her attention was focused on the writhing bodies that moved all around them.

Julian touched Isaac's arm and spoke just loudly enough to be heard above the din.

"We must be patient. Even a place such as this must eventually nod its head in the direction of the fable of Romance. They will play something slow and sentimental for these people, something to allow them to cling to one another, to whisper in a stranger's ear of their insatiable need. In the interim, you will go and bring us two brandies, as the service here is also a myth."

Isaac found his way to the nearest of the bars and ordered. With the brandies, he returned to the area that he had occupied with Julian, but he was no longer there. He looked around and located him prowling among the crowd in such a deliberate manner that it made Isaac uneasy. At last he returned to Isaac's side and took his drink.

The better part of an hour passed with no words spoken between them. This was not a place where conversation was encouraged, or even necessary. This was the domain of the pleasure-senses. Everyone knew why they were here.

Then the predicted moment arrived, and the token slow song was cued up. Isaac couldn't help but smile as dozens of couples took to the floor and embraced each other with a sophomoric tenderness that belied their previous gropings. Julian made his move.

He walked to where the blonde was shaking her head at the requests from the men around her. He bent gracefully at the waist, spoke into her ear, and held forth his hand. She took it and rose to join him in the dance.

Julian moved fluidly, leading and guiding her with an apparent familiarity. It was lovely to watch them. With some effort, Isaac fought off the warmly-intrusive memories of dancing with Lessa. This was not the place to sully those visions.

When the song ended, Julian took her hand and led her back to where Isaac stood waiting. The three of them found a cushioned corner and sat down.

"This is my acquaintance, Isaac Bloom. Isaac, I would like to introduce Erica Nance."

She held out her hand and Isaac shook it lightly, absorbing her beauty. His curiosity was mixed with a growing concern for the woman's safety. What did Julian have in mind? Was Isaac going to be forced to witness something more horrible than he had in St. Louis?

But the conversation seemed normal enough, and eventually managed to ease most of Julian's concerns. The three of them discussed the city and the music and other related trivialities. There was easy laughter, and some flirtation forming between Julian and the young woman. The question of why they were here, in this particular club, hung like an unspoken code of thieves' honor between them. There was to be no questioning of the motives of dark need.

After about an hour Erica excused herself for the lady's room. When she had gone, Julian looked at Isaac and spoke in his direct fashion.

"She is dying. There is little time left for her."

Isaac was incredulous. "Did she tell you that while you were dancing?"

"No. I am not certain if she knows it herself, though I suspect she does. That is the likely reason she has ventured into a world such as this. She has no place here. But I would venture that she has a terrible need to know a range of experiences before she vacates this life. It cannot be an easy thing to know that you must die soon. It can only be harder to know that you never will. When she returns we will learn her story."

Isaac mulled it over. It was too incredible. Did the reading of minds come with the vampire tool box? How could he possibly know that this young lady was dying? Yet his previous victims bore a silent testimony to his methods.

Erica returned and smiled warmly as she resumed her place between them. Julian asked her if she had ever tasted Cognac and she shook her head. He offered his glass. She hesitated for only a moment, then took it from him, inhaled the aroma at the rim, and drank deeply. The two men looked on as she coughed and gasped in surprise.

"Wow. It doesn't give you much warning…the smell, I mean. It has such a mellow warmth on the nose that you would never suspect the potency. It seems like it's just going to slide right down your throat," her eyes lingered on Julian's as she spoke, "but it builds up this hot friction and catches fire halfway down. By then it's too late to do anything except sputter like a rookie."

Isaac could see that she was blushing. And the warmth in his own cheeks affirmed that he was, as well.

"Have another swallow," Julian suggested. "There is a trick to drinking Cognac that makes for a quite pleasurable experience. But we won't go into that right now."

"Thank God," Isaac thought. "There have been too many reminders already this night."

She drank some more and slid the tumbler back into Julian's open hands. Now a silence fell upon their group…a solemn sense of expectation. Erica seemed to be preoccupied with her own private thoughts. After several minutes Julian spoke again, his voice a kind of caress.

"Erica. Why are you here tonight?"

Isaac was taken aback by the abruptness of the question. He looked quickly at the woman and noticed a difference in her facial expressions. They were composed and entirely free of the tensions that had masked them earlier. Of course! She drank from Julian's glass. There was some sort of bond between them now. Like the one that he shared with the vampire.

She looked down at her folded hands and replied softly.

"I was lonely. I came here for some escape."

"Escape from what?" Julian probed.

"From death, I suppose. I have lymphoma. They tell me I'll be dead in six months."

Tears welled up in her eyes and began to fall heavily, like the words from her lips.

"I'm twenty-two years old. Can you guess how unreal it is to hear myself say that I am dying? I lost both my parents two years ago in a car accident. I haven't even recovered from that yet, but here I am. My friends still call me to join them here or there. I still read the papers and watch the news. The world is going along just fine...life continues all around me...but I am no longer a participant. I am waiting for the end. That's all. I don't even know what life is all about, really..."

Isaac could hardly bear to look at her. His heart, which had lost much of its pity for the plight of strangers when compared to his own, was suddenly overwhelmed with sorrow. Her words, "I am waiting for the end..." she couldn't imagine how they pierced him with sharp daggers of relevance. He glanced at Julian and could see that his manners, too, had changed. There was a surprising softness in the eyes that were resting upon the young woman. This man was a killer. He had taken the lives of untold hundreds of miserable human beings. But here he was, obviously moved by the tears of a woman he had just met. How could the night possibly contain any more drama?

Isaac pulled his handkerchief from his pocket and handed it to Erica. Julian took her other hand and raised it to his lips, pressing them against the smooth palm. Then he looked into her eyes and spoke with such warmth that even Isaac felt enveloped by peace.

"My dear. There is no permanence to suffering. There is a balance. I promise you that this is true. The terrible beauty of life is nothing more than an enduring lesson in love. Whatever else you may feel that you have missed, I can see that you have learned this single, most important thing. So rejoice, and let go of your fear. In a moment I am going to kiss your lips. When I do you will forget the anxiety that our conversation has caused you. But you will retain the sense of hope that you now feel. And tonight, when you lay down for sleep, you will dream of your parents, and you will find faith that they are waiting for you."

He leaned forward and lightly brushed his lips against hers. They lingered there for a moment, and Isaac was so moved by the poignancy of it all that he had to look away. He rose and walked to the bar as clouds of warm rain gathered in his throat. As he stood waiting for a fresh drink, Julian walked up beside him.

"It's time for us to leave, Isaac. Our little 'experiment' is concluded."

"But what about Erica?" he asked, struggling to find her among the crowd.

"She will be all right. As all right as any of us can ever be."

He turned and retreated quickly from the scene, leaving Isaac to follow like a reluctant employee.

Out on the street, Julian paused as if to consider. Isaac felt a tremor of dread race along his spine. Was this to be the moment his fate was decided? Julian turned to face him.

"Return to your hotel. Dress for dinner tomorrow night and meet me at Arnoud's at eight o'clock. Good night, Isaac."

Again, he walked away. Perhaps it was his secret knowledge of Julian's true identity, but there was a noticeable difference as he made his way through the shuffling tourists. Julian carried his separateness on pressed, somber shoulders, like a burden of great weight. It was a familiar carriage. He recognized that gait as his own. He and the killer seemed to share certain characteristics. That knowledge dug at the very fabric of Isaac's previously-ordered universe.

He turned in the direction of his hotel. He tarried for a moment, considering the dying woman, Erica. Part of him wanted to return to the carelessness of The Zoo and bring her from there. But that was no longer his role. The rescuing of hearts, the drying of tears…these were personal failures. And they were forever behind him. Besides, he had his orders.

As he neared his hotel, he encountered another submerged emotion. One that he was sure Julian would disapprove of. It was a simmering hatred, one that Isaac had tended and stoked and looked after for some fifty years. The man was a murderer.

He preyed on innocent human life. Isaac had known many such monsters in the past.

"This must be remembered," he told himself as he climbed the stairs to his room. "I will not be seduced by his apparent concern for the dying. People have suffered at his hands. And I will not forget..."

The night had been an epiphany. But there was too much to digest in one evening. He went straight to bed and didn't awaken until well past noon the next day.

Chapter Eleven

By eight-thirty that evening, the two men had been seated and were sipping at the excellent wine Julian ordered before they even considered the menu. It was a Burgundy, from the Volnay region. Like Isaac, Julian often ordered the meal around the wine, in contrast to the habits of most diners.

"This has long been considered the most feminine of all the Burgundies," Julian explained, unnecessarily, but Isaac found himself hanging on every word. "If you prefer the elegant to the powerful, if your idea of a perfect evening includes jazz, moonlight spilling across the overstuffed couches on the front porch, and a loyal dog curled at your feet…if all you desire is the company of a good and loving woman, this wine is the official libation of lovers everywhere."

Julian seemed to be in high spirits, as if he were starved of company. The thought struck Isaac with a thunderbolt of humor, and he began to chuckle, despite his desire not to do so. Starved of company. Of course. How could he not be when he killed and consumed everyone that he met? Ha-ha-ha. "Oh my," he thought. "In a minute he's going to ask me what's so funny and I'll have to tell him and then I'll really be in trouble….ooohhhh, ha-hahaha…come on, Isaac. Get a grip, man!"

Julian only smiled at Isaac's amusement. "A wonderful wine, wouldn't you agree?"

Now Isaac was close to full-on belly laughter. "Oh yes, I can't recall a more convivial wine. Goes right to the head. That's what I love about the Burgundies. One minute you're staring down the barrel of life's futility, and half a bottle later you're dancing on the table in your underwear. Here's a great ad campaign," he picked up the bottle and pretended to read from the label. "Village de Volnay…it WILL tickle your fancy….ooohhhheeeeheeeehhaaahaa…"

Julian was grinning broadly now. "Perhaps we should order. You must be starved."

That was it. Wet, mirthy tears sprang to Isaac's eyes. A long-restrained humor and laughter poured out of him. "Ooohhh… hehehe. Good idea. OK. I'll have the ecrevisse aux oeufs, and my discriminating friend here will have the rack-of-human-flesh. Rare, of course…woooheeheehee…oh, boy, I'm a dead man…"

"Calm down, Isaac. Anxiety is mostly an intellectual thing, but it can manifest itself in a variety of ways. Your sudden slant of humor is a reaction to your forced reevaluation of reality. It's perfectly understandable. Now, shall we order?"

Isaac regained his composure. But there could be little doubt that his own mood was linked to the vampire's. Their conversation remained pleasant and humorous. Small talk dominated the five courses of the meal, but Isaac was brimming with questions. He would have to be cautious. His own history made him keenly aware of the sensitivity requisite when making personal inquiries. Particularly where such longevity was involved. He opened with the easy stuff.

"And how long have you been in New Orleans, Julian?"

"Too long, I'm afraid. I came here to visit many years ago and was simply enchanted by the city. I returned shortly thereafter to set up a residence. But soon I will have to look for a new home. I am becoming too familiar here. And more than any other form of carelessness, that can prove most dangerous."

He paused and took a long swallow of his wine. Isaac could see that he wanted, perhaps even needed, to talk.

"I absolutely love the history and the multi-cultural experiences here. This city is among the last of its kind in America. She has such an authentic feminine mystery. The summers can be trying. But in the spring the rains come, and the empty streets lend a dark reflection to the city's moods. After Mardi Gras, when the flow of tourists has ebbed and the narrow alleys and hidden courtyards of this sacred town have regained their almost-religious, Southern slumber, I will walk the streets into the latest possible hour. My clothes and my skin absorb the river fogs that shroud the Quarter in secret enigmas. Beneath that gray, misty shroud, the city is transformed. You can not guess, until you are almost indecently close to a thing, what that thing has become."

Isaac was feeling more comfortable about asking those personal questions. And Julian was ever more responsive.

"You understand, of course, how incomprehensible this is? I am dining with a man who is— if I understood you correctly— more than six hundred years old? You are history itself. I wonder if you wouldn't mind sharing some of that history with me?"

Julian smiled. "I admit that it has been a very long time since I have shared any of my story with anyone. But you and I seem to share some of life's tragedies, Isaac. Perhaps we will both learn something from such a venture. What would you like to know?"

Isaac thought for a moment. The story of Scheherazade came to mind. If he could keep the vampire talking long enough, who knew what might happen? Maybe Julian himself would find reason enough to spare Isaac's life.

"Quite frankly, I would like to hear everything you're comfortable sharing...right from the beginning. How did this happen to you? What have you seen? It's all so fascinating to consider."

In this, Isaac was quite sincere. Over the inevitable Remy XO, Julian began his story. History.

"The year was 1383. I was born outside Arles, France, to a poor farming family. Have you ever been to that part of the world? It is a lovely land in which to be young. I try to return there as often as I can, even though the ageless memories wear upon my heart. It is more hauntingly beautiful than even Van Gogh could do justice to. Our farm was not far from the Mediterranean coast. On those glorious days when the winds come fresh from the south, you can inhale the sexy, salty fragrance of the sea. It must have been days such as these…I'm sorry, I mean, those. It's so interesting when I look back at the past that I am almost transported there, with all its vivid colors and scents. Anyway, it must have been such days that siren-called my younger brother, Robert, and me to later adventure.

"Only a year separated us, and it was all that did. In the isolated and rural landscapes of our youth, we had by necessity become the best of friends. We fished and hunted as a team, and learned to cook together in our mother's kitchen. Our family tables were not always heaped with bounty, but our parents instilled a strong appetite for love. And the love of family was a kind of sacrament of itself. When we offered our prayers before meals we would join hands and each, in turn, would speak aloud our sincere gratitude for our food…and for our kin."

Julian paused to refill their glasses, sat deeply back into the cushions of his chair, and continued.

"The familial friendship, which my brother and I never took for granted, carried easily into our twenties. As young men, we made our first journey to the exotic, mythical kingdom we knew only by name and reputation: Paris. Oh, how clearly I can recall that adventure. Each stride of our horses' hooves toward that ideal seemed to electrify us with a more heightened sense of anticipation. The vibrancy of our youth coursed through our veins. And then we were there. For both of us, it was the first exposure to the full palette of sensual pleasures. Paris was the sweet, juicy essence of the forbidden fruit. It is very much like New Orleans, that way. I have been told that they are sister-cities, and that seems most appropriate to me. For two young farmers from the simple fields, Paris seemed part of an alien galaxy. But those stories are for another time. We returned to Arles after a fortnight as men of the world. We swore ourselves to bachelorhood and looked forward to our next sojourn. Even after these infinite years have rushed beneath the bridge of time, it seems that only a single sun has set upon that happiness."

Isaac was fascinated. And he knew that more fascination was in store.

"It wasn't until I had turned thirty that I began to reconsider my vows of hedonism. There comes a time when the quiet comfort of a country home seems like a come-true dream. I had all that I needed there in Arles, except for a loving wife, and perhaps a son and daughter to cook for on Sundays. I imagined my brother and I raising families together, always as confidantes and comrades, a fellowship to carry us far into our winter years. So I set about to find a kind woman who could comfort my spirit as well as my flesh. But it was an unsettled time. Far to the north, beyond the pleasures of Paris, the King Of England had become even more obsessed with French soil than the English had been for the previous decades of the Hundred Years War. Our own king, Charles, was hopelessly insane. So it fell upon the citizenry of France to protect our homeland from the arrogant expansions of the English. Robert, who loathed the English as much as anyone, took an officer's commission in the army. Three months later, out of a need to look after him, I did the same.

"It was 1415. That summer had been particularly hard on the people of France. Henry was a big fan of the old scorched-earth game. He left little but flames, ash and sorrow in his wake.

Certainly no food, nor the ability to grow it. But the winter was coming and it was time for his armies to retire beyond the Channel. The October rains had swollen the rivers and made them impassable. The English dog was forced to take his troops much further inland than he would have liked. We had not defeated the English in battle for more than a generation. But the whims of nature made him, at last, vulnerable to our forces. And we intended to make him pay.

"We caught his fleeing army in the open fields of Agincourt. We had them vastly outnumbered, but foolishly allowed them to reach the cover of the trees. There, they were able to set their defenses behind a wall of Europe's finest archers…the surgeons of medieval warfare. We charged their position again and again, as though the sheer force of our numbers could withstand the black, quivering rain of arrows. They cut us to pieces. Robert carried three shafts of English Ash in his body before he fell."

Now Julian paused for several, silent minutes and swallowed hard at the warm brandy. He looked off into the near distance, recalling the carnage of the scene.

"We finally retreated, what was left us. And it's odd. I watched that field being plowed over just a few months later. I have always wondered at the richness of that next summer's crop. But on that evening, as the very heavens poured their grey misery onto that blood-soaked land, I learned the essential nature of madness. Under the cover of darkness, I set out to recover my brother's body, with the intention of carrying him back home to our farm. By now the English had retreated as well, leaving only the woeful cries of the dying behind them. I stepped over torn bodies, often stumbling among the corpses, searching the contorted faces for that one, beloved and familiar. It is such a dreary memory…"

Now Isaac could see that Julian was no longer enthusiastic about recounting his past. It was torturing him. After all these centuries he still suffered. Was there no end to the tenacity of grief?

"All the light had fled from the world. There has never been such blackness. The sounds that reached my ears were relentlessly maddening. I could no more hope to find my brother in such a nightmarish place than I could have found reason for our bitter defeat. I was succumbing to shock. At first, I hardly noticed the chill of the ground fog that crept in over the carnage. But gradually I began to notice that the sounds were changing. There was something terribly different. The pain-wracked cries of the dying had turned to shrieking calls for help. Those men were screaming in fear. But in their cries was something else. I had heard fear in men's throats before. But never this. This was new. This was horror. The blood drained from my withering heart, and I was filled with a sudden and shuddering foreboding. And rightly so, Isaac. Rightly so. I began to flee as best I could among the scattered limbs and gory remains of my comrades. Still the screams increased with the rolling mist. Then the most disturbing sounds of all came to my disbelieving ears. It could not be. This was the depths of madness. Dear God...what WAS that sound? It was the unforgettable symphony of a vast hunger being sated. Wet and voracious, and all around me. I stopped running and peered into the fog. As my eyes adjusted, I saw them. They were everywhere. The oldest and lowest form of night feeder, preying mercilessly on those who still clung to life. They were not like me, Isaac...not like me at all. Not like what I have become. They had embraced a gluttonous evil, severing their last arteries with humanity. They had become true monsters. And their only pleasure was the blood of the living.

"Now I began to flee in full panic. The ground was so mired in bloody entrails that I could hardly stay upright. It was hopeless. I was caught from behind and dragged down into the mud and the butchery of Agincourt. The thing was greedy, wanting my flesh as well as my blood. If it had drained my blood, as it intended, I would have gratefully perished with all the others. I would have gone to a merciful rest alongside my dear brother. But an unexpected rent in the clouds allowed the sun of an early dawn to peer through, and forced them prematurely from the killing ground. For the first and last time, I was saved by the sun. Changed into something I did not wish to be. Something I fought the urges of for years and years after. Something forever different and unacceptable to the world that I am forced to inhabit."

Now Julian seemed to withdraw deeper into the cushioned chair, and closed his eyes. His features were drawn and cold, causing him to look every year of his six centuries. Isaac was, indeed, fascinated. But he was not moved to pity. There was little empathy. How could there be? Julian was a killer. Isaac and his wife had been victims of their own horror.

Julian's eyes fluttered open and he stared across the table as though he was disoriented…or guessing at Isaac's thoughts.

"You have opened ancient wounds, Isaac. I am willing, however, to suffer these memories if they will pry you from your stubborn blindness. I am increasingly of the opinion that we have been drawn together by more than coincidence."

He rose and laid a small fortune in cash on the table.

"But it is late, and I have matters to attend to. Return to your hotel and try to sleep. We will resume the vampire's history tomorrow night in front of the cathedral at nine p.m. Try to bring an open mind with you, won't you? Good night, Isaac."

CHAPTER TWELVE

The next night found them partaking of a solemn stroll. The joviality that had begun the previous evening was noticeably lacking. They meandered along the Moonwalk, overlooking the river and the lights of the towers that glimmered upstream. Isaac stared off across the swiftly dark water to the far bank and the twinkling lights of Old Algiers. Julian seemed to be gathering his words carefully, like each one held an unalterable meaning that, once uttered, could never be reclaimed.

They had met at the entrance of the St. Louis Cathedral. Julian had appeared to be hovering just inside the doorway, causing Isaac to replay all the vampire myths in his head. But Julian had merely shrugged his shoulders, stepping out of the shadows and into the pearl-bloomed night. They came to an empty bench and Julian motioned for them to sit. The vampire resumed history. His story.

"As you might imagine, my life had changed abruptly. In the space of a few hours, I had lost my dearest ally and all my previous connections to a normal mortal existence. I left my home in Arles and took to the roads. The English had become emboldened in their advances, and the Hundred Years War raged on. Occasionally, I would allow myself some measure of revenge on an English encampment, slipping in in the dead of night and draining the life from as many as I could before the sun. Guerrilla warfare took on a new meaning, and my tactics may have been the first to qualify for the term 'Black Ops.' But I could already sense that the killing, especially under the guise of 'revenge,' was just an excuse to satisfy a growing lust for blood. I was playing with fire.

"But then a most amazing thing happened. There have been very few times during the course of this curse that I have been grateful for. But meeting Joan of Arc was one of them."

The breath left Isaac's lung in a whoosh. He stared at Julian as though he had just sprouted feathers. "I'm sorry. It sounded like you just said you met Joan of Arc?"

"Met her. Yes. Became a kind of confidante for awhile. And helped her, in my fashion, to end the siege of Orleans."

Now a silence, so rich and electric, settled over them. Julian allowed the news to settle in. And he realized that he had never once spoken those words to anyone. The next thought reminded him that he hadn't spoken most of his recent confessions to anyone.

"There was a growing excitement, especially on the part of the farmers and the peasants, about a girl, an illiterate teenager from Domremy, appointed by God to drive the English out of France. You see, as is the case in every war, the poor had suffered most brutally, had lost so much more than any Duke or Dauphin ever could, and Joan was one of them…come to relieve their disproportionate misery."

Isaac had recovered his ability to speak and was abuzz with enthusiasm. "But…but…what was she LIKE, Julian?"

The moods of both men suddenly lifted. Julian laughed out loud at Isaac's exuberance. It was good, very good, to talk about Joan. There had not been anyone on the face of the Earth, for some time, who could speak with any authority about her, after all.

"It was easy to meet her. In 1429 she was traveling, darting here and there in hopes of meeting the heir to the throne, Charles VII. No matter where the road led her, the end of each day always found her in the local chapel or church, where she would spend hours before retiring to sleep. Some would tell you that Joan spent those hours in prayer. But as an intimate observer of some of those nights, what I can tell you is that she didn't speak aloud and she certainly never asked for direction or blessings of any kind. Mostly, she would lie on the stone floor, stretched out there like an antenna, arms and legs reaching in opposite directions, and she would listen, like you and I would listen to a stream, or birdsong in the forest. Entranced by the vibrations that seemed to run through her, she would twitch and kick her legs, and run her hands across the stones. It was after one such session, maybe the third or fourth I had quietly observed, that I approached her. I was quite certain that, to a woman who had been visited by St. Michael and who was on a first-name basis with God, my own strangeness would barely raise an eyebrow. Joan of Arc was a highly sensitive being, and my sudden presence in her life was not only accepted but might have even been anticipated."

Isaac could not stop his head from shaking, back and forth, back and forth, trying in vain to assimilate this story…to find some point of reference in his own experiences thus far that could make some sense of this surreality. To no avail. This was the very definition of uncharted territory.

"You asked what she was like. I can tell you that as a vessel for the divine, none have been more worthy of it. Oh, don't get me wrong. She could be rough, and even coarse. At Orleans I listened to her hurl insults at the English as casually as one might hurl a stick for some cur to fetch. But off the field of battle, she was the very picture of grace and humility. Perhaps she was keenly aware of her illiteracy, because she spoke very little, and only then when the words were tuning forks from Heaven. And there were words

I wouldn't speak, either. I never mentioned the word vampire to her, only that I had certain talents, gifts, if you will. I came to understand that she saw me as an angel of death, sent from God Himself, to aid her in her holy task of driving the English from French soil. It was a role I took to quite naturally. One that I relished. And while this will provide a jolt to your system, I have reason to believe that the secret words she spoke to Charles to persuade him to give her an army had something to do with her claim that she had a secret weapon…an angelic ally, capable of wreaking dark and sudden terror on the enemy."

Isaac was practically feverish. His body trembled, caught in a tension between outright disbelief and some sort of almighty gratitude for the hearing of such an incredible tale. He scanned the features of Julian's face, looking for some sort of nervous twitch that would give away the lie. But Julian, as always, was supremely composed. He returned Isaac's gaze with serenity.

"And that is how we saved Orleans. She called on me only once. I was to enter the city by whatever means I chose, and lay waste upon a couple of their commanders. But the most decisive part of the plan was to allow myself to be caught in the act of liberating the English dogs from the burden of their mangy lives. I drained the blood of the last of three captains and then cried out loudly for the guard. Two of them entered the bed-chamber and immediately froze with the predicted icy fear and horror. In their disbelief I was able to make an easy escape. The next day, possibly because they didn't want to face the announced assault by the Maid of Orleans (perhaps a sorceress in her own right as far as the enemy was concerned) or maybe because they did not want to spend another night among the fanged shadows of a city they had no right to, the English quit Orleans. And I quit France. I made passage across the Channel to the British Isles. I began to wander again."

Isaac's eyes practically bulged from his head. "But Joan was burned only a couple years later. Weren't you there? How could you not have been?"

"I was there."

The words seemed to wrap around them like a shroud, echoing off the walls of some crypt where the last mourners refused to leave.

"I could not stand in the sun and watch her burned, but from deep within the shadows of the keep, I could see the courtyard below. I could see the flames, and I could smell the flesh as they consumed that sweet child. That night I allied myself with the darkness and became a shadow, so that I could go into that courtyard and comb among the ashes for anything that might remain of Joan of Arc. Alas, there were ONLY ashes. I scooped up a handful and placed them in my pouch. Then I left France for another three hundred years."

Julian unbuttoned the top buttons of his shirt, reached inside, and pulled forth a kind of amulet or locket. "This is all that remains of the Maid of Orleans."

Isaac stretched out his fingers, tentatively, as though he were about to touch a flame, and took the amber-colored orb into his hand. His head began to spin. Julian tucked the locket away and placed his hand on Isaac's shoulder to steady him.

"Should I continue?"

Isaac could only nod his head.

"For the next century, I wandered the Celtic moors of Scotland and Wales, living—if one could call it that—among the rubble and ruins of decaying castles in lonely, isolated regions. In 1532, I settled for the next 128 years in the ruined fortress of the cliff-top castle of Carreg Cennen, in the heart of Wales. It was the perfect setting for the vampire stories you would recognize from folklore and Hollywood caricatures. The interior buildings were in complete disrepair, but the walls and towers were intact. Its greatest feature, however, was its sub-level maze of rooms and tunnels. I was able to secure the peace for my needed retreat from the day, without worry that some curious hunter might stumble upon my slumber. During this period, I came as close as I ever would to becoming a kind of monster. I lived to eat. Each night I would ascend into the towers and gaze out from that wind-torn summit across three hundred square miles of territory. This was my feeding ground. The lights of the distant villages beckoned to me like a servant's bell to the evening meal.

"Within a decade the legends had begun, of yellow-eyed jackals sweeping over the moors, craving the pale young flesh of the village children. I never left a body behind me to be recovered. Nonetheless, the grizzly accounts of my nocturnal ambitions were posted in every village that fed my need. Wildly-horrific descriptions of limb-severed virgins found still writhing in their final anguish. The decapitated remains of a wandering cleric, his white-knuckled fingers vainly clutching at the blood-spattered Bible on his breast. Such were the nightmares of a simple people.

"In truth, I was nothing more than a transparent soul, drifting along on the currents of perpetual night. There was no fellowship for me. By necessity, I was a stranger to everyone, and becoming so to myself. Once or twice, I naively attempted to converse with my victims. But this only complicated matters, and I realized that the process was best carried out impersonally...for all involved. I was related to those who had made me. And it was becoming more difficult to recall what I had once been. The seasons rolled like a wheel. The cycles of life and death played on without me. The only notice that I took of time was in the way that it lingered like a malicious jailer, always reminding me of my sentence.

"Eventually I was forced to leave my castle. The villagers had taken to abandoning the night altogether. As soon as darkness settled over their fields and their farms, they locked themselves away behind bolted doors and posted watchmen at the gates. I realized that I would have to take up residence in the city if I were to have a reliable source of protein and still be able to maintain my anonymity. So, in 1660, I took a house in London. I was ready to surrender that tiresome struggle with myself. My dreams were in crimson. I had lost so many of my memories. All of their colors had faded with the forgotten sun. It was vanity to think of myself as still human.

"London was a strange counterpoint to my existence. I was back among the great diversity of people and ideas that thrive in the petri dish of a large city. Being out among them each night, I could almost feel that I was part of their society. Passing them on the thoroughfares along the Thames, looking into their eyes, recognizing the common threads of their humanity...some of them would even smile at me. And I would have to quell my eager desire to follow after them like a stray cur in need of a home. Often I would sit on an empty bench along the river and just watch them pass. As the hours fell away beneath the slow-moon death of the night, their numbers would inevitably dwindle to a scuffling, solitary soul...the three a.m. man that I have known in every town I have called home. It's odd, but that lone, solitary figure seems as cursed as I am. I wonder at how they disappear... into a place that is mostly painful recollection of some estranged family, or the sudden-waking-longing of a heart-torn wife."

Julian rose suddenly, like some voltage had swept through him, unseen by Isaac, but certainly noticed. For Julian, it was the realization that he was coming to another difficult part of his story. One that was mixed with gratitude, for sure, but also with a sense of loss that he could not hope to recover from if he existed for 600 years more. "Let's stretch our legs...and perhaps our hearts and minds, Isaac."

They continued upriver. Outside the Aquarium of the Americas they found a beer vendor and bought a couple of Dixie long necks before resuming the leisurely pace of their stroll, and the leisurely pace of the vampire's story.

"In London I continued to walk the narrow line between my blood lust and my diminishing humanity. I knew that it was a zero sum game, and I had no hope of winning it. As time passed, with less and less reason to act human, I would eventually become one of those Hellish creatures I most feared becoming. Five years passed in this manner. Five years during which I considered returning to some faraway place where the people weren't so recognizable in their vibrancy…in their joy for life. It was, in fact, my self-disgust that brought awareness to my unused sensitivities concerning the vitality of life, as it compared to the sluggishness of impending death. Once I realized I could tell the difference, my reality began to shift once more. You might say that I was evolving.

"Then one night, as I was stalking my usual feeding ground in London's West End, I came across the frail figure of a woman slumped in an alleyway. My senses weren't as well-defined as they are today, but I could tell that she was near death. She was an obvious choice for my need. I bent over her, and just as I was lowering my mouth to her flesh, a group of people rounded the corner and rushed towards me. I rose hastily, prepared to flee, when I heard a young woman cry out, 'There she is. That gentleman is rendering her aid. There may yet be time.'

"I stood aside as one of the men knelt over the woman and began to administer to her. The man was a doctor. And the woman who had taken my presence as a sign of assistance was the sister of my intended supper. She had gone for help when her sister had suddenly collapsed, and had returned before I could feed. She introduced herself as Clara and thanked me for showing her sister compassion. I tore my eyes from the prone figure at my feet and looked closely into Clara's face. I realized at once that she was the loveliest woman I had ever seen. My nerves were suddenly a rash of rawness. More striking than her physical appearance, though, was the way her eyes examined my own. There was a depth of soul in those twin pools. She looked at me with a kind of familiarity. You never forget a look like that. As though all of time, and all the world's events, had been a meaningless prelude to that singular acknowledgment. For just a moment, I wanted nothing more than to hang my head in shame and beg this woman for pardon. That was all that I needed, Isaac, just that one look. That seeing. And from that moment forward I wanted to live up to the faith, and the expectations, in those eyes.

"I assured Clara that I had done little, only checking her sister's vitals before they returned. The men gathered her sister in their arms to carry her to Clara's home some few blocks away. She informed me that her sister had been ill for several days, and that the doctors weren't quite sure what to make of it. I was invited to join them and offered tea for my 'trouble.' I nearly declined, of course. The situation was beyond awkward. But there was something still human inside me that responded eagerly to Clara's gentle nature. As I hesitated, I realized just how wretched and lonely I had become.

"So I did go with them…following along behind them, feeling my difference weigh upon me like gravity with each heavy step. Passing the corners, each one another opportunity for escape. But suddenly there we were and Clara was actually inviting me into her home—me, the bloodthirsty killer—and I stepped across her threshold to a new life.

"Over the course of the next week I would return at nightfall and sit with her as she kept vigil over her sister's labored dreams. We became close, conversing as I had never had the occasion to converse with a woman. She was so kind and warm, so much like the benevolent sun that it was often painful to look at her. And even as her sister lay dying in the next room, Clara was able to reach out through her own loss and salvage the part of me that had been in such mortal peril only a few weeks before.

"Can you comprehend, Isaac, how long it had been since someone had cared for me? And how unworthy I felt? Let me make it clear; Clara never learned of my secret. Yet her feminine intuition informed her well of my differences. I suppose it was her faith that assured her of my innate goodness, and that one day all would be revealed. When her sister succumbed, it was me who she turned to for solace. Our nights were fused. And they were the loveliest nights in a time so lovely, and so brief in its effulgence, that even after all I have endured I am forever grateful to have known…and to have loved…her."

They finished their beers in silence. Walking, pausing to take in the crush and the flow of the people around them on Decatur Street. The hawkers were out in force, pimping t-shirts and over-blown Mardi Gras beads. Music flooded the air like a monsoon. But both their minds were on a love affair….each on his own. A love affair swept away by time's relentless tides but still felt as keenly as an arrow sent just now into the cavities of the heart.

Julian willed himself to continue, taking little joy in the thought of the chapter yet to come.

"Even in my previous life, I could not have hoped for a woman like Clara to love me. As my feelings for her became entangled in my reality, a sense of hopelessness set in. Surely, nothing but tragedy could come of it. Like all lovers, I wanted this love to last forever. But I alone had proof of that improbability.

"It was during this time that I began to feed exclusively on the sick and the dying. Whatever could be done to improve my bond with humanity, I was willing to attempt. I would become a better man for Clara…a man she could love for all time…"

He laughed. A poisonous, cynical sound choked off as soon as it started.

"I loved her. But I was seeing that things were nearly as bad now as they had been before I met her. Now I had something entirely foreign to deal with. Hope."

He glanced at Isaac and his next sentence was almost a whisper. "Love demands a profound courage…but I suspect you know this. This may be the one of the reasons why modern relationships are not grounded in permanent commitment. No one believes in forever anymore…

"It was insanity for me to harbor any hope that this might be a thing that could carry us both through all the sadness and loss of the world. I was to learn how little love has to do with what we think of as happiness. In the meantime, I hadn't kissed, or even held her body against mine, yet. Then, one night, as we were walking along a moonlit path in Hyde Park, an occasion happened…one that caused my heart to flood its long-arid banks. We had just climbed over a small rise in the path when, out of nowhere, two snow-white Arabian stallions came charging along the lane directly at us. They thundered past us, close enough to touch. I pulled Clara aside into a narrow stand of black poplars. Moments later, two drunken barristers, still in their powdered wigs, came stumbling along in pursuit of their horses, cursing and yelling at one another. 'You damned fool! I told you to mind that branch! And what swashbuckling-fantasy were you attempting when you decided to leap onto my mount, you bloody sot?'

"Clara had never been so close, so warm that she seared my heart, branding it forever her own. In our private glade, my arms remained protectively around her. Even though the danger had passed, neither of us had moved. Then, breathlessly, she took my hand and placed it between her breasts, and whispered, 'Can you feel how frightened I was?'

"I could feel her heart trembling like a winter bird beneath my hand. I could hear her blood singing. For just a moment I had to fight back a hunger I had neglected so as to spend my nights with her. My very soul cried out for nourishment. A nourishment much more satisfying than blood. With centuries of longing, I kissed her. Her need seemed to be as infinite as my own. My hands fumbled at her hips, which were moving with a passion that I allowed to consume me. She raised the folds of her skirt, and my hands followed. The ties on her bodice seemed to unravel on their own, allowing me access to the bounty of her bosom. I suckled there first, her turgid points of pleasure swelling beneath my ravenous attention. And then I suckled her everywhere. Every single nerve ending, every pearl of her pleasure…I tasted them all. It was a new kind of satiated hunger. When I finally melded my body into hers, for that glorious moment that it lasted, I felt the almost violent release of all my loss.

"For the next several days we sampled love's myriad pleasures. And for the first time in my life I knew the deep satisfaction of 'romance'. We did all of the silly things that new lovers do. One morning, pre-dawn, after a long and glorious night of sensuality, I drew a hot bath, lit candles around the clawfoot tub, and poured a bottle of Champagne into the bubbly depths. This surprised her until I explained that the warm water would open her pores, and her body would 'consume' the heady beverage through a million eager orifices. And while we sipped on a second bottle, I caressed her thick, dark hair into a luxurious lather. I sent the soft edges of my tongue into her ear and nibbled gently along her lobes. I teased my self with the pulse along her throat, turning my hunger into an erotic meditation. "How is that bubble-buzz, my love?" Her oohs and ahhs were sweet music to my heart. It was the single, most satisfying night of my long life.

"And now my decision was made. I would tell her everything. She would understand. I would never subject her to the nightmare of the vampire's existence. But I would love her through all the years of her mortality. First, I would prepare my words carefully. This was not a casual bit of news I would be offering.

The passion of those nights needed a calm tempering. Our love affair had caught fire. A month later, after much procrastination, I informed her that I had been called away from London for several days, a fortnight. But that I had important matters to share with her upon my return. She embraced me eagerly, and wished me Godspeed.

"I took the coach to Dover and spent several nights in contemplation. I thought it all through...what to say and how to say it. I anticipated her possible reactions. And on my final night in Dover, I went into the chapel there.

"Yes, Isaac. I know you have been curious since you saw me in the doorway of the cathedral this evening, and hearing my comments about observing Joan in her element in church and chapel. I can go wherever I wish, so long as it is under the cover of night. It is the sun that I cannot tolerate, not churches. In fact, I spend a great deal of time in church. My hours of worship just happen to be a little different."

They had wandered back beside the river. The flow of the dark currents seemed to be an inspiration, a source of energy that Julian took some solace from.

"I prayed. I actually prayed for the first time since Agincourt. I prayed for a miracle. I asked the so-called loving God to allow me the salvation of love. To grant me, if not mortality, then at least the chance for mortal peace. I prayed for the sunlight colors with Clara...for maybe, perhaps, a family. Such folly. I returned to London the next evening, still clinging to my embryonic hope. To my eternal horror, I had been betrayed. The city was sealed. The puzzling death that had claimed Clara's sister was nothing less than the second coming of the Black Death. The plague. It was ravaging London. I had been gone for two weeks but it might as well have been a century. I exerted some persuasion and was allowed to enter the city. Bodies burned in the streets among the revelry of the damned. The populace was strangely, dangerously calm. They had turned on one another, using one another, fulfilling long-stifled fantasies of violence and sexuality. I hurried to Clara's home and found her there behind locked doors, lying peacefully upon the bed we had only just begun to share. Lying there waiting for me. Her body was still warm. But I was too late.

One heart-heavy tear ran down Julian's face and dropped off his chin onto the sidewalk. Isaac found the distillation of tears, time, and space astonishing.

"Ahhhh. The pain of it still burns like white embers. I had implored the Heavens incessantly for an authentic experience of love. And it had been given to me…only to be snatched from my arms before I could even fully embrace it. How does a man reconcile this?"

Isaac took Julian by the arm and looked into his eyes. Not with sympathy, but with the kind of understanding that comes only from experience. He knew that, despite his own feelings, the story needed to find its conclusion. "The rest, Julian. Tell me the rest."

The vampire inhaled deeply of the night air.

"It was the most striking rebuttal to my prayers. I had tasted, oh so briefly, that peculiar tenderness that aches so fiercely for itself. Centuries of time and the innocent renewal of generations have come and gone. But the salt-pinched moments I shared with Clara were the high water mark of my life. And that is why I felt such deep hatred toward the God who had mocked me. Yes, I go to church. But for centuries I have gone only because I have nowhere else to go."

The sudden realization struck a chord with Isaac. Julian was right. There was nothing left for him in this world. No respite from the cycle of night and blood. How many prayers had the vampire cast out into the echoing silence of that cathedral, and places like it? How much time had he spent just waiting, longing for some reply that had never come?

A deep and abiding silence settled over them once more. Julian's story had become a kind of song, a piece of music, the notes and the pauses all creating the rarest melody. Isaac could only hang his head. So they did share love's tragedy. The loss of the one most beloved. The loss that can never be healed, only endured.

Julian spoke hoarsely and interrupted Isaac's train of thought.

"Hell is a hope all its own. Return to your hotel, Isaac. I will come for you tomorrow night."

He started off, turned abruptly and spoke once more. Then he was gone, leaving his words to linger on the air behind him.

"Pray for me."

CHAPTER THIRTEEN

Later that night, as he stared up at the shadow-patterned ceiling, Isaac replayed the vampire's story in his head. He could hear the cracking pain in Julian's voice, like the razing of old, haunted rooms, as he had discussed Clara's untimely death.

It was clear that grief followed after life like a shadow. A broken heart could never truly mend. It was destined for internment with the bones and dust of our mortal losses; even then, it might lie there, in the quiet decay of the tomb, its sorrowful energies reverberating, crying out into the dark, hollow void. This haunting energy, Isaac deduced, is what we have come to know as ghosts.

Evan Connor had once compared that suffering loss to a kind of mining operation…like a great, leviathan machine, tunneling deep into the secret, sorrowed recesses, gouging away at the diamond-coal vitality of a heart. Once the machine of loss had moved on, leaving a quarry pit of ache for the essence that had been taken, the deeper, wider trench was ready…ready only then for the new jewel of eternal love.

Julian still carried that terrible soul-yearning for his Clara, just as he did for his Lessa. Isaac was willing to concede that the vampire had shown him something about the infinite nature of love. But hate had an infinity of its own. And in the absence of the comforting warmth of love, hate could fill in quite nicely with a sustaining flame of its own.

Isaac's thoughts drifted back to Auschwitz, and to his friend, Patrik. Patrik had embraced and tended the coals of his own searing hatred for the Nazis. It had kept him alive as their other friends had perished, one by one. Patrik's German was fluent and flawless, and he taunted the sluggish ignorance of the guards by confounding them with their own language. His subtle and incessant insults were delivered in such a way that they could never be quite certain that was what they were. They came to respect Patrik's rapier tongue, even keeping their distance from him when at all possible.

The intensity of Patrik's hatred radiated like a stoked furnace. And it helped stabilize the roller coaster of despair that Isaac was prone to each day. For the first seven months, Isaac had no word of Lessa's fate. Then, one of the guards struck up a friendship with Patrik. It was one of the camp's many paradoxes. The two men of opposite realities would spend hours over a chess board. It was through the favors of that friendship that Isaac finally learned Lessa had survived her initial processing.

The news had caused an unsavory reaction in Isaac's character. He became a kind of lackey, scurrying to perform trivial favors for his captors at every opportunity. To Isaac's way of thinking, if he could somehow make himself valuable to the Nazis, perhaps if a critical moment of uncertainty should arise over the question of Lessa's fate, his actions might have a favorable influence. It was the same fantasy-fueled mindset that had driven his insanity in the ghetto. And Patrik was incensed. He approached Isaac one night after the camp had bedded down.

"What, exactly, are you trying to accomplish with all these circus-monkey antics? If Lessa could see the way you grovel and lick at these fascists' boots she would weep great tears of shame."

"I don't care, Patrik. I'm doing it for her. Perhaps someone will pull some strings in her favor if it should be necessary..."

"Isaac, my friend, you have not yet come to terms with what these people are, and why we are here. You were in denial in the ghetto and you remain so here in the midst of our extinction. All of your subservience will not stay a single hand from falling on our people. Far better for you to become anonymous than to stand out with your eager compliance. Come on, Isaac. You are too smart for these dangerous games!"

But Isaac could not—would not—agree. His humility was expendable. He would sacrifice any and all for the slimmest possibility of benefitting his wife. His friendship with Patrik suffered. The two surviving members of their Warsaw fraternity became estranged.

It seemed that Isaac was destined to play the ill-fated role of the misinformed, vague-hunched gambler who would wager all, time after time, only to come up just short. He never guessed at how his failed bids would tear even further at the tatters of his remaining faith. But fifty years later he could lie in the dark with the accumulated baggage of his regrets and look back clearly along the path of his failures. It was too late to amend his hatred. Julian had come along after many years of ill-defined, randomly-targeted resentment. And he supplied Isaac with a tangible object for it, just as Patrik had once had his.

He suspected that the vampire already knew this. Why else would he have gone into such intimate details of his past if not to try to solicit empathy? He had purposefully divulged the most pitiful aspects of his life. But Isaac could only feel the sort of leniency that one might offer the hungry children of some Third World backwater...nothing too taxing on the heart. His was a convenient sympathy that could easily be over-ridden for the deeper gratification of his hatred.

He only hoped he could conceal the true depth of his feelings. It was one thing for the vampire to guess at Isaac's distaste, but if Julian were to comprehend Isaac's hatred, Isaac might find himself in a situation that could only end poorly. He still felt little fear at the prospect of death. But he was certainly able to choose wisely between the two options.

He turned his thoughts to Lessa, and finally drifted off to sleep with her voice humming a nocturne to his dreams.

At eight o'clock the following evening, Isaac responded to the knock at his door with some dread. Julian was there, and he wore a grim expression. He also wore the clothes of a man accustomed to physical, if not emotional, comfort. Linen trousers rolled once at the cuff, revealing canvas shoes laced twice by black laces. His shirt was white broadcloth, rolled as well, revealing massive forearms, and a wrist adorned with a precision timepiece with a Swiss name.

They didn't speak, but wandered the streets for an hour, absorbing the fluid energies of the Quarter. At the base of the equine statue in Jackson Square a group of young people passed a bottle of muscadine among themselves. Julian smiled at them as they passed and one of the women offered the bottle. He accepted graciously and drank with a healthy thirst. Someone was playing an acoustic guitar, and playing it well. The night was warm, sexy, and alive with stars.

Isaac was taken aback. Julian handed the bottle to the old man and Isaac drank in spite of himself. He had the sensation that he was being played like a familiar instrument. Julian looked at him carefully and asked, "Are you ready to talk? Are you ready to remove some stones from the quarry?"

Ah. So he was, indeed, understood. He nodded and followed Julian for a block up Royal and into a modest cafe. Isaac glanced back over his shoulder at the kids in the square. He was certain there was a woman in that group who loved lullabies.

Julian ordered raw oysters and Dixie beer for them both, and they talked briefly of sports and music and food. Once again, it was an oddly normal conversation. Until Isaac asked how it was that Julian seemed to enjoy "normal food" like oysters and salads, etc. Julian replied that his appetite for such things was genuine. Food was enjoyable. But only human blood could provide the necessary sustenance. Then, gradually, Julian began to steer the subject matter to fate, to purpose, and to the evolution—or lack thereof—of the human species.

Now Isaac was certain that the vampire was fully aware of his revulsion. Julian was intentionally leading the conversation. He wanted to make a point or two.

"You are a stubborn man, Isaac. I have a need to make you understand me better. I admit, finding ourselves in one another's lives is something I don't completely comprehend myself. But I have no doubt that there is some purpose to it. We will, and I stress WILL, learn the dimensions of this mystery, together."

Their refreshments arrived. Julian swallowed a quarter of his beer and resumed.

"Here is the truth of it…contrary to your prejudices, I am not corrupt of spirit. I am not evil. The corruption that you fancy in me is nothing more than the reality of my nature. Just as the scorpion must use the poison in its tail, so must the vampire feed on the blood of the living. For six hundred years I have struggled to maintain my humanity in spite of my affliction.

"After Clara's death, I very nearly succumbed to the primal desires of the Old Ones. I abhorred the God who had so brutally betrayed my impassioned prayers. Clara's death was my final break with the delusion of salvation. Now I was free to satisfy my cravings as my appetites dictated.

"But try as I might, I could not rid myself of the deeper feelings that Clara had awakened. Her innate goodness had given life to my own. If I wished to sustain my love in loving memories— and

I so desperately did—then I could not become a monster. Clara's love, which I had wished upon like a star, could only survive through my own evolution. It was a long shot, and I knew it. But I believed that, somehow, if I were worthy, I might just see her again. Do you see how it is? That the long-lived intensity of our grief might be the only authentic validation that certain love can reach into infinity?"

Isaac looked away. Such words coming from a vampire! Yet he couldn't deny the turbulence of the emotions gathering in him like a coming storm. And Julian poured it on.

"So I made a conscious decision to refine that sense I already possessed…a sense inherent in all predators. I learned to locate the old, the weak, and the dying. This is what I tried to show you in that club with Erica. Certainly, I could choose any victim. With the possible exception of lovers, whose aura is too blinding, I can feed on anyone. But, for the past couple of centuries, I have targeted the dying exclusively. That is why I prey primarily on the homeless. From the predator's point of view, they are the natural choice. Society's discards. The sick, the insane, the hopeless. They are all there, in every city in America, and in ever-growing numbers. I do not want for wretched victims. And, whether you accept it or not, I often relieve them of the burdens their lives have become."

Isaac had sat passively with the tempest gathering inside of him. The vampire's last remark triggered his explosion.

"Euthanasia!!?!" He immediately lowered his voice when several sharp glances stabbed at his outcry. "You imagine yourself a mercy killer? Do you honestly believe that you are doing these poor people a service? Perhaps you should poll them first. You might be surprised to find that they prefer their lives, as miserable as they might be. You remind me of a barbaric group of murderers I encountered some fifty years ago. They too thought that they would do the world a great service by exterminating all non-Aryans. Very noble of you, Julian. You should be applauded."

He had spit the words out like venom, in one breath. He gulped air, then beer, and glared into the darkening eyes of the vampire. Several minutes passed before Julian responded with icy control.

"Listen to me very carefully, old man. In a twisted, worldly sense, I may well be performing a service. Not necessarily for the sad creatures that fall to my hunger, but for your uncaring and self-absorbed little society. You have cast these poor creatures aside long before I stumble upon them. But the crux of the matter is that, like you, I have no choice but to feed. I have no choice but to seek sustenance. I do, however, have a choice over whom I will feed upon. And I have chosen the most natural path for the historical predator: targeting the weakest creatures in my territory. It may not be noble, but it is certainly not evil. Particularly when you realize that the choice of who I am has been taken from me."

Isaac started to voice an objection, but two raised fingers from the vampire silenced him. Isaac could see turbulent anger bubbling beneath the black orbs of his eyes. Julian continued with subdued intensity.

"I have, at times, looked bitterly upon this species that I must depend on but can no longer belong to. I consistently show more humanity to this herd than this hypocritical mass you call mankind. You, of all people, should appreciate what I am saying. You are a victim of one of man's grossest atrocities. I kill out of need, Isaac. But I have observed the perverse pleasures that man derives from the act. So many righteous wars. The indiscriminate slaughter of innocents, Genocide. Assassination. And these are the acts of governments. The legal horrors that some privileged High Council awards itself, but punishes in its own citizenry. Your species practices layers of evil that I am incapable of understanding."

Julian stared down into the dregs of his beer as a gypsy would stare into a crystal sphere. "This humanity…it twists and warps its youth from an early age, then medicates the very imagination out of them. How many of your children are depressed, angry, suicidal? And then ask yourself how many of them are understood? Whatever genius they might once have possessed has been eradicated by your mono-culture and all that is left is the pursuit of wages and lifelong mediocrity. Can you give me a single example of how the West prepares its citizens for any kind of moral enlightenment? We condemn one another for our differences but think nothing of the assembly-line-for-sameness that the 'civilized' world has become.

"I recall one of many troubling days…when the lesson of sameness was renewed and repeated like the easy rhymes from a determined nanny…nearly two hundred years ago. Just outside of Vienna, a city that boasted of its culture, and its appreciation for the genius of 'art.' It was a darkly rainy twilight, too miserable even for mourners. I stood above an open grave, alone. Peering down into that ditch, that pit, strangled with the frustrated emotions of it all. There were a dozen shroud-wrapped corpses, jumbled and tossed down together like garbage…a stinking chaos of 'final rest.' One of them was Mozart."

He paused again, swallowed hard on his now-warm beer, and called for two more. When they arrived and he had drained half of the fresh one, he went on.

"I could bore you with stories like that for a month…a lifetime. Time and again I have watched as a handful of men and women from their respective generations have labored against the narrow visions and expectations of their societies, only to be disillusioned and cast down by mass conformity. The unique is abhorred. And the sickness that your world perpetuates is treated, not with healing and compassion, but with punishment. Your prisons overflow with your refuse, just like your streets with your homeless. You strap living human beings into monstrous contraptions of voltage and anguish and you call it justice. But the melting eyes and the burning flesh smell more like revenge. It is an ancient odor. I have inhaled that stench the world over."

He paused and looked deeply into the old man's eyes...to the very edge of Isaac's soul.

"In fact, I detect traces of it right now."

Now Julian was whispering, and Isaac found himself leaning involuntarily forward in his seat.

"You want revenge, Isaac. This is your curse, just as I have mine. You want revenge so badly that the craving for it sustains you like food. And you want it of God Himself."

Isaac jerked back into his seat and stared with wide eyes at the vampire's remarks. But Julian wasn't finished with him yet.

"You think of yourself as faithful, with your pious hypocrisy. You are so typical. There is but one shred of greatness left in you, and one only. Your love for your wife is your truth. But it is not enough to save you because your hatred is too strong."

"No!" Isaac had found his tongue again. He was answered once more with harsh stares from the other patrons. "You know nothing of my love, or of my hate. You grasp at straws of cliched human weakness to give credibility to your own delusions. It is you who is unsaveable. You have made truths from your lies, but they persuade only yourself."

Julian was unruffled. "Then enlighten me. Tell me YOUR story, Isaac...from your own lips. And we shall learn the truth together. I suspect that the truth is a grave you have been throwing dirt over for many long years."

The vampire had commanded, and Isaac was now compelled to reveal the most intimate aspects of his life.

CHAPTER FOURTEEN

"Julian, you know that what you are demanding is difficult for me. If I must speak these things, then let us leave this place."

"Yes, alright. We will take the streetcar to Audubon Park, and we will talk there. Come."

He rose and the laid cash on the table. They walked to St. Charles Avenue and caught the car, then jumped off near Loyola University and walked into the shadowed interior of the park.

Isaac noticed the scarcity of vagrants, and Julian explained.

"Most of them gather in City Park, or stay on the roam in the Quarter before retiring under the wharves along the river. This park is too close to the tourist sites and is swept by the police at regular intervals. It wouldn't do to have the tourists tripping over those who have no place to go but who have to go somewhere. As you must have discovered, I don't prey on the homeless in this city. There is an old wisdom that cautions not to build your out-house next to your pantry," he commented without humor.

When they had walked as far into the park as they could without beginning to walk out again, Julian stopped at a bench and motioned for Isaac to sit down. Time assumed a fullness, and each minute of silence weighed on Isaac's narrow shoulders like a stone. Finally he could postpone it no longer and the words began to take the shape of Isaac's shattered life.

"My story. Perhaps it is one of faith…or the lack of it. From childhood, even when my uncle would talk about the dangers that faced European Jews, I would allow my thoughts to wander to happier places. My uncle was political. Not involved in Polish politics, but well aware of how they affected him, his family, and his people. He was constantly warning and reminding all of us to be alert, to keep our noses to the wind. But I could never imagine the things he warned of, even though so much was already historical fact. These things had not touched me personally. So I was able to maintain a foolish belief in a worldly sort of good nature. I was an apathetic human being.

"Early on in my life, my story becomes the story of Lessa. It is a thing that I have considered from infinite angles. Lessa was so perfect for me, so complementary of my flaws and strengths. At first I thought of myself as the stronger of us. That was wrong. I was wrong about many things.

"Lessa understood me better than I knew. My 'strength' was really nothing more than a kind of self-delusion about the reality of things. It is easy to be strong and brave when you cannot see the hammer swinging at you from behind. And Lessa's 'fear,' which I spent a great deal of time trying to console, was actually wisdom. Here is the irony. When the matter finally played itself out and the Nazis came to Warsaw to prime our people for the 'Final Solution,' Lessa's fear evaporated and was replaced by a resolve that one could only acknowledge with awe. My 'strength,' on the other hand, eroded quickly into a hopeless, pitiful despair.

"Lessa and I had grown up together. For all those years, I had listened to her poems and lullabies….so lyrical and sweet… and terrified of the night. Midnight, dark storms, lullabies, and nocturnes. These were the canvas of her intuitive dreams. I had come to look at Lessa as one might attend to a frightened bird. I showered her with attention and affection, thinking that these would comfort her misgivings. But all she ever needed was my acknowledgment of the truth. She wasn't afraid of the Nazis. She was terrified of my indifference.

"It wasn't the Nazis who inspired Lessa's courage. It was what happened just before they came into our lives. It was our marriage. That bonding in love was the final piece of life's complex puzzle for her. With the discovery of true love she came into a season of renewed faith. That faith in the enduring power of love over fear liberated my wife. While fear bound me in layers of chains, Lessa's faith in love allowed her to soar above all the mortal madness.

"It was a faith that, try as I might, I could not connect with. When the Germans came to Poland, I began to struggle with incredible guilt. Lessa had asked me, begged me, only a year before to flee from Poland with her. Once again, my denial, to use your word, kept me from seeing the true danger. I was able to convince her of the folly of her ideas. But then one morning we all awoke in the ghetto and premonitions of catastrophe began to mock my every waking hour. I withdrew deeply into myself, into a disgusting little world of self-loathing and self-pity. I was unworthy of my new bride. I had failed her. And more...I had doomed her.

"I would close my eyes at night and pray for the mercy of sleep. Instead, I was tortured by Bosch-like visions of those filthy beasts with their eyes and their hands groping eagerly at my Lessa's beauty. We were so unarguably at their disposal that they commanded life and death, comfort and pain. If their whim was a bullet in the brain of a child or the brutal rape of a young wife, it was done.

"Here is where my madness began. The ghetto was a staging area. We all knew it. Just as we knew that the random terror of violence wasn't really quite so random. The Nazis systematically weeded out the very young, the elderly, and the sick. So it became conducive to pass oneself off as healthy, robust, and in the prime of life. Old men who had walked half-erect for years struggled to right themselves, to conceal the limp of an ailing wife or an infirm mother. Terror raged like a great fire around our people. You could have argued that the world had become too grim to support the laughing dreams of life. But here they were, contorting themselves, going to extreme lengths so that they might pass the Nazis' tests for a brief reprieve…for their very survival.

"I could not reconcile any of what I was seeing. It was obvious to me that God had turned his back on His faithful followers. How, then, was anything to save us? We were on our own.

"But Lessa tried. Dear God, she believed. And she almost reached me on one rain-threatened afternoon, in a field outside the city. It was a lover's field. We had been picnicking. One of those last days before the ghetto roundup began. Lessa was, once again, speaking words of comfort and reassurance to my deafness. She was so patient, Julian. The storm finally broke as we lay there, and I began to gather our things to flee the deluge. But she reached out and took my hand…and pulled me back down to the blanket to make love in the rain. I suppose that she sought to reconnect me to the wild wonder of life and love. And she whispered something, words that vibrated and echoed through the years of sorrow. I didn't understand them then, and I ponder their meaning to this day. 'Eden was never tame…'"

Isaac paused, as if hearing the words for the first time. He peered off across the dark expanses of the park, imagining a pair of trusting lovers there. Lost as he was in his reverie, he did not notice the raw currents of electricity that surged through the suddenly-jolted vampire. Julian made a conscious effort to calm the breath that had suddenly expanded in his lungs.

"In any case," he continued, "a few weeks later the Nazis gathered all Jews into the ghetto. All of my fears seemed justified. If I had known then that there was an even darker night before us, I would have worked harder to find my way back to her…to make the time that was left to us more special. As it happened, I very nearly went completely insane when they herded us like livestock onto two narrow rails bound for the ultimate despair… Auschwitz.

"We were separated immediately upon arrival. For the next seven months, I survived without any particular will or desire to do so. But word finally reached me that Lessa had also survived the processing. I wish that I could explain in some sort of new, startling language how such information can work upon the mind. It wasn't an altogether welcome revelation. For now, I began to worry about her all over again.

"I had brought Lessa to that place. Subsequent fallout from that frame of mind was my unhealthy desire to secure her safety at any cost. I ingratiated myself with the guards. I was willing to perform any task, any unholy act that might work in Lessa's favor. You have to understand. I was a weak, lice-ridden Jew, the lowest of the low to our captors. Somehow, I needed to get their attention and, hopefully, their sympathy.

"I volunteered as a sonderkommando…that is, I removed the bodies of my people from the gas chambers."

Isaac swallowed hard, his hands trembling uncontrollably, and Julian could see that the old man had reached a place where old, incriminating memories had been buried for a long time. Isaac was venturing back into Hell.

Chapter Fifteen

"In the hierarchy of the death camp there is nothing lower than the sonderkommando. The work we did was so foul, so repulsive, that we were shunned by our own people. Even the Nazis could barely stand the sight of us. And of course they would despise us. While many were forced into the role, there were just as many others who, like myself, volunteered in the hopes of currying favor...mostly the favor of life.

"When the new trains arrived and the lines formed to shuffle off to the 'showers,' we, the untouchables, would take our place just outside the doors, as the doomed filed past us. We dared not look at their faces, for fear that we would cause them undue anxiety. If they could believe that they were being deloused, as they were told, they wouldn't suffer as much. Then we would close the iron doors behind them. For the next several agonizing minutes, as the gas hissed and filled the chamber, I would die with those voices that reached us from the other side...the children crying out for their mothers...until the last muffled cries were stilled. And our terrible work would begin.

"I did this work. And I accepted the consequences...the contempt that was spit at me, the random beatings in the barracks, and the total isolation from my fellow Jews. The autumn of 1944 was a harsh one. The camp was running at peak capacity, fed by the trains that converged from much of Europe. The gassings and the ovens, day and night. I would stand beside the window at night as the barracks slept, and watch as the tongues of flame rose up from the tall, black stacks, licking at the dark, hungry lips of a night that seemed to have settled over the entire world. The ashes would sting my eyes and settle upon my tongue. My people. But I could no longer allow myself to care. I had made my choice. I had offered up the sacrifice of my conscience, had burned out all human feeling, for the slimmest of chances that doing so might somehow benefit my wife."

Isaac fidgeted in his seat. His feet tapped at the ground like his fingers on his knees. He knew that he had no choice about whether to tell the next part of the story...the part that would reveal his utter unworthiness to be called a human being. But the telling of it was still an act of inner violence. He hadn't even spoken these words to Father Connor. Finally, like something being spat out into a clogged and overflowing toilet, he brought the words up from the deepest, darkest part of himself.

"This work...that wasn't the worst of it. After removing the bodies of those women and children, of our elders, I had to take them all to a tiny, claustrophobic room where a guard stood over me as I removed any gold fillings from their mouths. I would stand there, the corpses shoulder-high around me, dragging them all in their turn onto the table...and then. Oh, God. And then...I had to search the cavities of their bodies for any hidden valuables... the little babies, still clutched in the arms of a stranger because their young mothers would have been spared as workers...and... and they made me search them, too. The bastards thought our people so hideous that we would hide our jewelry in the rectums of our children....Ahhhhh! It was worse than death. My shame should have caused my body to seize up, and fall dead among the withered sacks of bones around me. Or, at the very least, the disgust of the guards as I did these things should have compelled them to place the barrels of their Lugers against my shaved skull and send me directly to Hell. But my body refused to die. Long after my soul had fled, I continued this work, as numb as a winter pond. Saying this now, I still want to die from my shame. How had I strayed so far from that lover in the field, in such harmony with his beloved, to become this sub-human so despicable that he could rob the fillings from his people's gaping mouths? How can I ever justify it? You must relieve me of this life right now! Lessa's love made her an angel! And my fear turned me into a horrible, terrible monster! Kill me, Julian! Please!!!"

Bright, heavy tears filled the lines of Isaac's weary face. Julian had to turn away. This was more than even he had witnessed. After six hundred years he was no longer surprised by man's callous brutality, but he was also not jaded to personal tragedy. The story was ripping the very heart from both of them. But Julian knew now, beyond any doubt, that it had to be purged from the old man. As difficult as it was for Isaac, the vampire could now see how it all fit so perfectly together. Someday, Isaac would as well. He touched him gently on the shoulder.

"Not yet, Isaac. Not yet. You must continue. This must be done."

Isaac wiped the tears from his face. After several minutes, he gathered himself, nodded, and drew a deep, ragged breath.

"Another four or five months passed and we began to hear whispered, tenuous rumors that the Russian army was advancing toward Auschwitz…and that we might be liberated any day. But now I came into a new world. One with a landscape that was nearly as terrible as Auschwitz. Hope."

He looked up at Julian, who nodded in understanding, then continued.

"I had never struggled with hope before because I had no faith in things working out. This went all the way back to the apathy of my youth. Now I needed faith and there was little to be had. So, in my fashion, I set about to find it. I knew that I, personally, didn't deserve anything. But Lessa did. So I grabbed hold of faith in her name. And I was determined that I would see it justified. Since there was nowhere else to plead my case, I knelt down into that most awkward of positions for a man of no faith, and I attempted prayer. I prayed with intensity and with sincerity. I prayed incessantly. Walking, standing and kneeling. I prayed over the gassed bodies and I prayed when sleep betrayed me. I prayed until my throat was raw and my lips were dry and cracked. The days passed. As the war drew to its grizzly climax, the Nazis somehow managed to increase their slaughter even more. Each day that I waded through the suffocated bodies, searching for that familiar angelic face, I held my breath.

"But my fragile, embryonic hope had learned to walk. I actually began to make plans for our future. A family. I had heard other rumors as well. Palestine…it would be our sanctuary from all the ugly savagery of the world. Lessa and I would be pioneers. Zionists. The future was coming, and Lessa had been right. Auschwitz held no power over love. Of course! Love was a power that worked through, and beyond, mortal circumstances. I was beginning to see the truth of Lessa's faith.

"Now I jumped through every hoop the Nazis could devise. I had convinced myself that it was me, my actions and my prayers, that were saving Lessa from those lethal vapors…and from the blazing ovens that had already made ashes of so many other dreams.

"Then, on a cold, bright afternoon, just after the New Year of 1945, the guards called for volunteers to turn the fields outside the village. My hand went up, as always. I remember the unease that seemed to penetrate me like the cold…" He looked up again into Julian's face. "Have you ever had that peculiar feeling? When everything is too quiet…like the whole world is holding its breath because something significant is about to happen? Like the very clocks don't want to budge, for fear of rushing into something that can never be undone?

"The sky that day was as blue and fragile as a robin's egg. I stooped to retie a bootlace when I noticed a large crow glide low over the field and land ten feet from me. It stood there, peering off at the forest bordering the clearing. I followed its gaze to the trees, then looked back to the bird. A hot, fluid anguish rose suddenly in my throat, just as eight gunshots rang out in succession. The crow beat its wings heavily against the sound, and I watched it rise into the air until it became just a black punctuation mark, a period against the sentence of the blue sky. I was still staring up into the heavens when the guard came and took my arm, and returned me to the camp."

He paused again and swallowed against the spools of wire in his throat. There was a drought forming on his lips, and he longed for a drink.

"That night, Patrik came and sat beside my bunk. He didn't speak. But he had brought the old man, Viktor, with him. Viktor had been spared from the ovens because of his rare gifts with the violin. All through that terrible night, Viktor played the Nocturnes of Chopin while Patrik held my hand. It was Lessa's favorite music..."

Isaac stopped and looked at Julian, but Julian was looking away once more. And for a long while the two of them sat still, heads turned in different directions as their hearts recalled the same tune.

"Lessa had nearly made it. She had come so very close to being vindicated in her unwavering faith. Where had that faith wound up? Was it in a trench, a shallow grave in the woods outside the camp? Was her faith soaring up there with the crows, looking down from the heights, from a place where everything on earth was small and patched together without seams...without madness? Where was she? Where was her faith that seemed to mock all the violent hatred, that placed all that human cruelty in the margins of a greater message? Where was that undying resolve that I so desperately needed now…now that I had sold my very soul?

"When the Russians arrived, just two weeks later, I was all but dead myself. A corpse that wouldn't lie down. I had eaten only what Patrik could force into me of his own meager rations. I weighed ninety-seven pounds, and could barely raise my hands to shield my eyes when the big, Russian trucks with their blazing lights entered the gates to signal our freedom.

"I was numb with loss. Patrick wanted to find the nearest refugee camp and eventually make our way to Palestine. I didn't care one way or another at first, but I had to return to Warsaw before anything else. Lessa and I had buried our wedding rings near the wall, and I wanted to retrieve them if at all possible. I could not have accomplished it without Patrik's help. He never once turned his back on me…even knowing what I had done, and how I had shunned him for the amusement of those butchers. It had all come to nothing. But Patrik was true.

"So I returned to what was left of Warsaw, and that ghetto…for one miserable day. The Germans had flattened the place to crush our gallant and futile uprising. But I was able to find the rings that we had exchanged in some other world, in some other time. Then I left Warsaw without looking back.

"Patrik and I went our separate ways. I had decided to scour the refugee camps that were spread our across Eastern Europe, just in case Lessa had survived. Patrick could only shake his head. 'Isaac, you will never let go of your fantasies, will you, old friend?' We embraced and he set out for the Promised Land. He died three years later in Israel's War for Independence. He died a free man, fighting for his own homeland."

Isaac slumped back against the bench and blew a long, exhausted whistle from his lips. Another lengthy silence enveloped them. Then Julian rose and began to pace back and forth in front of the bench, considering.

"There is more," the vampire whispered. He stopped and peered down at Isaac, who was trying his best to shrink into the bench. "You have revealed much. But nothing more than one would tell a doctor, or a priest. Now I am commanding you. Tell me exactly what you felt when your wife was murdered."

Isaac could hardly breathe. His eyes darted about like a trapped animal. There was no escape.

"Damn you..." he muttered between clenched teeth. "I have told you how I love my wife. I was reduced to nothing when she was killed. Don't you understand? The bond between us was such that, though I didn't actually see her die, I felt it as if it were my own death. Doesn't that tell you how I felt?"

"Let me be more blunt then, Isaac. Who do you blame for her death?"

Now Isaac was visibly agitated. He clenched his teeth together, unwilling to utter the words that he knew must surely damn him. Julian rose above him like an angry master commanding a stray. "Speak, Isaac!"

"Me! I blame myself! Please, stop this! I am responsible for her suffering. And I had no right to hope after my mistakes had led her to that place. I had no right..."

"Everyone has a right to hope!" Julian interrupted him with an angry waving of his arm. "Man is nothing without it. There is nothing noble in hopelessness. You hoped as any man would. But your hope was..."

"Betrayed!!" Isaac cried out the word with fifty years of anguish. "Yes! He kept her for all that time...forced her to endure nearly two years of that horror...only to take her at the very last moment before our rescue. He is no loving God! He mocks us, toys with our hearts. We are inferior little creatures for His perverse amusement. I prayed. I made promises. Was it so crucial to

His plans to take her as He did? Was it too much to ask that love might actually triumph over that God-forsaken evil? What does God know of love? Lessa could have given lessons to His angels!"

Isaac was standing now, shaking with the rage that he had suppressed for decades. He counted to ten, and then to ten again, trying to regain some composure…enough to keep from shouting.

"Is that what you wanted to hear, Julian? Did you need to hear my angry words directed at God, when you know that He is the only hope I have of seeing my wife again? Yes, I have been betrayed. And I live with an uncomfortable situation. I am forced to depend on the same God who has already denied my prayers when I needed Him most. Does this prove your superiority over this pathetic little species? Can you go out tonight with a clear conscience and feed on another wretched old woman? Yes, I have my hate. And it may well keep me from the dream that I have guarded for fifty years. But how close are you to fulfillment? Do you even have any dreams left, Julian?"

Now it was Julian's turn to sit down. He hadn't expected Isaac's words to sting like they did. He knew that Isaac was wrong. Mostly wrong, anyway. But he also knew that Isaac's last question would haunt him for some time.

Isaac was breathing a little easier. As some measure of calm returned, it brought with it just the slightest remorse for what he had said. He wanted to try another tack.

"I became a Catholic after the war. Made a full confession of my anger towards God. I like to think that I was forgiven. But who knows? Perhaps even my conversion was just another old-Isaac tactic for covering the odds…trying to persuade without conviction. In truth, there has never been a real change in my feelings. I am still angry. I am still betrayed. I thought that I could cover it up. Or at least put my nose to the grindstone and, through sheer force of will, rid myself of this damned faithlessness. But you saw through me to the lingering bitterness. I suppose that I will die this way.

"If I have one saving grace, it is that I sincerely want to believe in an afterlife. I want to believe in that glorious reunion with my wife. Is it so uncommon to feel an angry betrayal at the loss of a loved one? Who is responsible if not this God that so many of us put our trust in? My anger is more passionate because I know too well what she suffered for so long before she met her violent end. If God is love, then He must surely understand my rage. And if He isn't love, then it was all for nothing, anyway.

"There IS a lesson I learned. One that was taught to me by Lessa, not by God. And that is that love, on some level, really is eternal. Somewhere, right now, Lessa is loving me. In our past, and possibly in our future, the living energy of our love is there for both of us. She can feel it as certainly as I do. I may never hold the warm, sweet creature that was Lessa, ever again. But what there is of our love remains beyond all that is transient and sorrowful."

He circled the bench where Julian remained sitting. It was time to resign himself to his fate.

"Perhaps there is no balance. My anger is great. Lessa would have argued love's superior advantage. Either way, I will know the truth soon enough, I imagine."

He looked down at Julian, and Julian raised his eyes to return the stare.

"Yes. But not tonight. Return to the street and wait for the taxi that I will send for you. It will take you back to your hotel. Tomorrow night, walk to the front of St. Louis Cathedral. I will meet you there at nine. It will be our final meeting. Goodnight, Isaac."

Chapter Sixteen

As Isaac's taxi sped him back to his hotel, at the frayed edges of the French Quarter, and a sleepless night during which he would restlessly recall the night's revelations, Julian stood alone beneath the arching canopy of a two-hundred-year-old oak tree. His heart and mind were awash in the agitation of mixed emotions. It had turned out to be one of the most incredible nights of his life. Just as he had suspected, Isaac had not come into his world by accident.

He had to proceed carefully now. There were great forces at work here. This was not intuition; Julian was in possession of physical proof. Fate had been busy in their lives. The thought brought a wan, fleeting smile to the vampire's lips.

But now what? What did this portend for him? Was it a promised answer to a long-suffering prayer? Had enough damned time passed that he could finally seek his rest? Or was it more mockery?

It was all too much to consider in his weakened state. He had not fed since meeting Isaac. The encounter with the old mortal had startled him, inspiring thoughts that had turned out to be a sort of prophecy of what had transpired tonight. Julian had fasted, like Christ and the Buddha in the wilderness, emptying himself of himself and preparing the hollow place for an epiphany. And wow, had the epiphany been delivered.

But now he must feed. His strength was declining noticeably. And he would have to feed here in his own city…a thing he had done on only the rarest of occasions.

An hour later, he was walking along the lakefront of the city's northern boundary and into the homeless haven of City Park. He passes silently among the sleeping forms, communing with the vitality of those he passed, until he found what he was looking for.

A very old man lay at the base of an anonymous Civil War statue. He was curled into a tight ball and breathing with rapid difficulty. Julian kneeled beside him and examined the drawn features of his face. Grey stubble dotted his jowls and head. He was emaciated…the weakest of the weak.

Julian pulled a handkerchief from his pocket. Wrapped inside it were a syringe of morphine and a rubber tube. He took the handkerchief and wiped the draining mucous from under the old man's nose. His eyes fluttered open at the contact, startled and widely afraid. Julian looked deeply into them and whispered reassuringly.

"It's alright. There is nothing to fear. I'm here to take you home. You have lived like this for too long, my friend."

"Are you an angel?" The old man asked with toothless awe.

Julian's hands trembled as he inserted the needle into the man's vein.

"Yes. And I am going to take you to a place of great comfort. Where the warm breezes blow through the windows of your room and someone you love attends to your needs. Now close your eyes, and we will go…"

After a few minutes, the aged features assumed a contented repose. Julian withdrew the needle, inserted the tube, and fed on the man's ebbing life flow.

Then it was over. He touched the man's head, rose and walked to a nearby bench, where he slumped into the seat. The old familiar feeling, experienced every single time, that pointed self-loathing, washed over him. The same story. It never changed. How many times had they asked him that question? How many times had he suffered their prayers? He was bone-weary of the routine. But he was convinced that it would be over soon. One way or another, it was all drawing to a close.

He leaned back and closed his eyes, then whispered a prayer of his own for the old, cold man on the old, cold ground.

The next night found the two somber figures occupying a bench in front of the alabaster facade of the cathedral. The iron-crossed spires rose beyond the lights into the dark heavens, casting their psychological shadows over the tourists below. Both men were caught up in their own thoughts—thoughts revolving around the mysteries and the meanings that such buildings implied.

They had sat there for most of an hour, passing Isaac's flask of brandy between them. Isaac hadn't slept except for two fitful hours at midday. Julian could have made a similar claim. But there was no fatigue, only a keen awareness of the jostling life all around them. He had never noticed so many couples in the streets. The lovers were everywhere, sharing their secrets, creating their memories. How had he missed them for all these years?

He had truly forgotten that love existed. It had seemed so natural to believe that, when Lessa died, all the stubborn, struggling love in the world died with her. And in the half century since then, he had never cared to look closely enough to see that he might be wrong.

Julian was putting the finishing touches on the idea that he was about to share with Isaac. So much had been revealed to him in the past few months, even before Isaac had stumbled onto his existence. And last night had revealed the final sign-post on their secret, parallel paths. The problem for Julian, now, was finding the courage to follow through. There was a high price yet to be paid for what he could only hope was an opportunity for that elusive, eternal, love. He would need all of Isaac's understanding.

But how was he supposed to manage that? Isaac had shown little inclination towards any kind of understanding, let alone vicarious forgiveness. He had heaped all the injustices that he had ever witnessed onto Julian's shoulders, making the vampire the focus of all his bitterness. This fact gave Julian pause. How could he do what needed to be done without Isaac's voluntary support? He sighed. He would simply have to forge ahead and hope for a breakthrough. He nudged the old survivor from his reverie and began.

"Isaac. There are some few things that we must discuss before this chapter in our lives can be closed. There are matters here that need your attention. Things that I cannot openly explain… things you must discover through your own reflections if they are to have the incredible impact on your life that they have had on mine.

"I want you to listen carefully with a wide-open heart. Two nights before our paths crossed in Atlanta, I had an experience that you should know about. It was here, in New Orleans. In fact, it happened inside that very cathedral you see before you.

"It was very late. Or perhaps it is more appropriate to say that it was very early. I had been walking all night in the rain, reveling in the storm that was scrubbing the city clean. In the distant sky I could discern the first purple hints of dawn. But I wasn't ready to retire the night quite yet.

"The rain and the empty streets had combined to inspire a vitality in my blood, in my bones, that I hadn't felt in years. The vibrancy of life was pulsing through me. I felt almost human again. I felt almost…holy.

"I left the Moonwalk along the river and, on a whim, I wandered here, and stood before that sacred shrine. I had not actually entered a church in several decades except out of curiosity. But that night I felt drawn to the place. Like a condemned heretic imploring some last-minute forgiveness, I entered the deserted sanctuary of St. Louis Cathedral.

"All along the rail before the altar, hundreds of burning candles were lined up like a brigade of hopeful soldiers. I lit one of my own and placed it among all the others. Then, with some stiffness from lack of habit, I got down on my knees and recalled my pleadings from that chapel in Dover. I had prayed for a miracle on that night three hundred years before. But not this time. I had learned, like all suffering humans, to lower my standards.

"This time, I prayed only for some sign…some small, token omen that I was not beyond the mercy I had tried to bestow upon my countless victims. I only wanted to know if I still somehow mattered to whatever God might be out there listening. I was quite wary of the hour. I would have to surrender to the morning soon. But I lingered there as long as I dared in my fervent longing.

"Then a sudden wind, the origins of which I could not guess, swept through the shadows and over the altar, extinguishing all the candles. But not as you would imagine, Isaac. They were not blown out all at once. They went out singly, one by one. Each in its turn, until only one candle remained. Mine. My candle, alone, continued to burn, seemingly brighter than it had before. The wind had departed.

"I stared at that candle in disbelief, unable to grasp its meaning. But slowly, like a curtain parting on some unscrupulous magician's trick, a dread realization crept over me. My prayer had indeed been answered. God was, yet again…what was your word?… 'mocking' me. Yes. He was telling me in no uncertain terms, just as surely as if He had materialized there before me, that my flame would never be extinguished. My curse was infinite.

"I rose from my knees in outrage, cursing and vowing never to seek such solace again. I understood His workings now. I could finally see, with more clarity than ever, how He lashes us time and again with suffering, and how our prayers become less meaningful, our expectations for love and happiness wither in the dust of His indifference, until we are left with the most stunted hope…which he finally crushes. Showing us once and for all that He is God, and we are merely chattel.

"It was everything you and I have discussed these past several days. It is the common plight of the suffering mortal who has lost much, and then lost even more in the pursuit of some sacred solace that doesn't come. Only the willfully-blind can claim some impossible, convenient 'faith' when it has never been tested. But to have faith after all has been consumed in the earthly fires, when every hope, every dream, has been crushed by the jackboots and the jailer…THIS is the faith forged like steel. This faith in love, alone, has meaning. And I have come to believe that it is the only faith that can persevere…that has the potential to break through from the blind-following of some *religious* faith to a direct and transformative experience of that love you and I call 'Divine.'

"But on that night I wanted to somehow get back at this loveless entity. I stood there in the near darkness, considering. And just as suddenly as my anger had consumed me, it was reversed."

He paused and looked squarely into Isaac's eyes.

"A single raindrop, from the storm that was just beginning to subside, somehow found a breach in that vaulted ceiling. It fell with perfect precision directly onto my candle. And my light…went…out.

"I was temporarily stunned. Then a joy, unlike any I have known since my days with Clara, began to fill my soul with a light of its own. I was not an abomination, after all. I was important… at least, important enough to not have been ignored in my request for a sign. There was still hope.

"I staggered out into the rain and I began to laugh. I didn't even hurry back to my home, although the sun was only minutes from its arrival and its warmth was already spreading through my body like a painful cancer.

"In my home, I waited. Since that morning, I have maintained a new kind of faith that— somehow—my reality was about to change. Yes, I have killed since then. But when you entered the picture, with your 'coincidental' discoveries and your familiar story of love and loss, I knew that the matter was at hand. I still don't fully grasp the details of the outcome, but I am certain of its prompt arrival.

"Isaac, we are both living, historical testimonies that there is barely enough love to balance man's hatred. Our credibility in this matter is beyond question. But I have come to believe that we have been blessed, yes...blessed...by our suffering, because it has been the burden of love that we have carried, and have never dropped. This means something. It may, in fact, mean *everything.* The time for redemption is very near."

With those words, the vampire rose and stared down at the still-seated Isaac. The old man stared back without fear, knowing that the moment had arrived, but incredulous at what he heard next.

"You are free to return to your home. My power over you will diminish in time, and you will be able to say and do what you choose. It will not matter to me, for I will have gone from this place. And your recent history, if you were to share it, would only harm yourself.

"We shall not meet again. But I wish for you the peace, and the reunion with your wife, that you have prayed for. I have come to respect you, Isaac. And I can very much sympathize. But you must lose your anger, forever. Your dream cannot possibly be realized so long as you carry that poison inside you. That dream is closer than you know."

"I want you to have something," he said as he reached into his shirt and drew out the amber orb, and the ashes of Joan of Arc. "Give this a special place in your home, as I have in mine. She's a saint now, and she belongs to all of us. I place her remains in your good, kind hands."

Isaac was speechless.

"Arrangements have been made for your return to Boston tomorrow. But for now you will return to your room and sleep well. Goodbye, Isaac. May you be blessed." Julian turned and walked quickly into the throng of tourists, who drew behind him like a curtain...not giving Isaac an opportunity to speak, to say goodbye...to say...

CHAPTER SEVENTEEN

Isaac Bloom sat in the comfortable wingback chair he had treated himself for his scholarly pursuits, in the days before he even imagined vampires. Four months had passed since Julian had walked away into the flowing-river-darkness of the New Orleans night. It was winter in Boston. And Isaac was officially retired.

The *Bhagavad Gita* lay atop a stack of books at his feet that included the love poems of Neruda, as well as a collection of Lessa's poetry and lullabies he had self-published for his own enjoyment. The title read, simply, *Nocturnes*.

Isaac's reading list had become predominately spiritual in nature. He was no more certain of his beliefs than he had ever been, but he was enthusiastically open to all of it. Asking genuine questions was a novelty he could get accustomed to. He was becoming a seeker.

But he was currently preoccupied with other thoughts… thoughts that were less than meditative. Evan Connor was due to arrive at any moment. And Isaac intended to speak to him of the bizarre events that he had recently been a part of.

The old priest's temperament had worsened in the months since he had confessed his waning faith to Isaac. He had been granted his request for retirement and replaced quickly, too quickly for Evan's taste, by a young, dynamic character not unlike the Evan Connor of 1945. Since then, he had faded into a self-imposed exile from most of his friends and followers.

It was risky to subject his unstable friend to stories of murder and ancient histories. But Isaac was prepared to gamble that the shock might help suspend Evan's spiritual tailspin. There was also the fact that Isaac needed the comforting words of the priest more than ever before.

As Julian had promised, the vampire's hold on him had vanished. At least, the compelling need to obey and protect him had vanished. But it had been replaced by the persistent feeling that there was yet some unfinished business between the two of them. There was something out there that Julian had wanted Isaac to understand. It was something that had come from Isaac, and which had altered the vampire's perception of eternity and eternal love. He had said that it was something Isaac must discover through his own reflections. Isaac had spent four months doing little else, with nothing to show for it but a growing anxiety that he was missing the point.

It was astonishing enough that he had been allowed to walk away. It was more troubling than soothing that the two of them had shared so many common experiences of tragedy and sorrow. But that was where the link needed to be examined. And Isaac had pored over his still-acute memories of those nights with Julian with a detective's inquisition. He was close, and the niggle-naggle realization of that was enough to drive him to hysterics. The knock came at the front door and Isaac rose to answer it.

"Come in, Evan. It's so good to see you, old friend."

The weathered padre entered the room looking considerably older than he had just four weeks earlier. The grey hollows beneath his eyes were basins of surrender. He slumped heavily onto the low divan and asked Isaac for a brandy.

Isaac fetched a tumbler and sat down across from him.

"How are you, Evan?"

"Alright, Isaac. You sounded more eager than usual to see me, so I hurried over as fast as these spindly legs would propel me. But I hope this doesn't concern matters of faith. I have retired from the shepherding of souls."

His voice was laced with a weary sarcasm. Isaac was stunned. This had progressed far beyond mere self-pity and doubt. It was bordering upon a total departure from all that Evan Connor had once held dear.

"I don't have much time to socialize, either, I'm afraid. I am in the middle of an epic project that is consuming my time in research. Something the old dinosaurs of the Church will find quite upsetting. I am shooting several holes in the good name of St. Augustine. Once a heretic, always a heretic, if you ask me. Man is simply incapable of changing his nature…"

Isaac was perturbed and cut him off abruptly.

"Evan, I asked you to come by tonight because I have something rather amazing to share with you. I need all your attention and open-mindedness…" He could hear the echo of Julian's words imploring him for the same.

He looked into Isaac's vacant eyes and wondered if he would have either. The wind had been building for several hours. Isaac walked to the fireplace to adjust the flue against the downdraft. He placed another log on the fire and returned to his chair. He was aware that the lighting was poor and that the firelight was adding a certain drama to the room.

"A moment ago you said that man is incapable of changing his nature. I am no longer so certain of that fact."

He looked again into his friend's eyes, then turned his gaze to the sighing logs and continued.

"During my last assignment for the magazine, I met an incredible man who has spent several decades trying to change his nature. He has, at least in part, been successful.

"I became involved in something that I have never told you about. As I sit here now, I find it too strange, myself, and I can only imagine how you will react. But I have to tell you, Evan. And I am going to need your help in sifting through the details to find its meaning."

He began to pace around the room. The moment had come to divulge the past month's secrets to his lifelong friend, and he was finding it more difficult than he had imagined. To make matters worse, Evan was taking him about as seriously as a parking ticket. He was stubbornly refusing to even allow Isaac the courtesy of a forum. There was nothing to be done except forge straight ahead, to meet Evan's stubborn inattention with a stubbornness of his own. Even would see the magnitude before much longer.

"Quite by accident…or maybe it wasn't an accident at all…I discovered…a series of murders, a recurring pattern that had been in place over the last half decade, and longer. Someone was preying on the homeless."

He paused and looked carefully for an expression of alarm on the face of the priest. But there was still only that vague comprehension. Evan hadn't yet made the emotional connection that Isaac was counting on. He continued.

"The fact of the serial murders was unsettling enough, and made no sense in itself. I mean, who would want to murder homeless people…for what reason? But all the other circumstances also seemed too bizarre to be true. I pursued the case myself so that I could verify what I suspected before turning it all over to the police.

"But the more I became involved, the more impossible it became to disengage myself. And the whole thing took on a stranger, darker tone than I could believe. So much so that I began to doubt my own sanity. It was during my investigations that I met the man responsible for the killings of all those pitiful people.

After spending a week with him in New Orleans, I knew that I would never be able to go to the police with my information."

It was obvious now that Evan was not going to become invested in the matter. He had made up his mind before he had even arrived that, whatever he was being summoned to, he was finished with intimate involvement in other people's problems. Even Isaac's. But he surprised Isaac with the extent of his apathy.

"This sounds too much like confession to me, Isaac. Wouldn't you like me to call that new kid who has taken my place? Perhaps he can lend a more sympathetic ear..."

"Damn it, Evan! Just hear me out, please. I don't know what all this arrogant indifference is with you lately, but I hardly recognize the man I have known for these past five decades. I have a genuine need to make you understand this matter, because I believe that by discussing it I might be able to grasp its true significance. It may seem odd to you, but through it all I have felt a certain purpose."

Now he hesitated again, acutely aware of the absurdity of what he was about to relate. He could hardly believe it himself. And he had lived through it. The situation was taking on the air of impossibility. But, amazingly, Evan was pushing ahead with his own point. He had obviously gone deaf in the past ten minutes.

"Did you know, Isaac, that St Augustine was a devoted practitioner of the occult sciences? And that he was quite proficient in astrology, before he gave up paganism?"

Evan continued with his original line of thought as though nothing out of the ordinary was about to happen...as though a ticking time bomb was not poised above his unsuspecting world.

"But he ran into a dilemma when he tried to reconcile the horoscopes for a pair of identical twins who had lived through completely different fates and circumstances. Because he was disillusioned with astrology, and only because of it, he turned to Christianity. Something that required less scientific evidence and more blind faith. Without those twins, we may never have even heard the name, Augustine of Hippo. But with the typical zeal of the newly converted, he set about discrediting paganism in all its forms, and they made him a saint for his efforts. I mean, this was the same hedonist that put God in his place; 'Grant me chastity and continence...but not yet.' Which just goes to show you...if you really want to be in the favor of God, you must renounce something and then wage a blistering attack on what you are renouncing. You must renounce the nourishing fountains of the hedonistic life and live in the withered desert of 'faith.' God just loves that prodigal son routine. For those of us who are uninspired enough to simply toil in His service every day of our nondescript lives...well. I suppose that quiet desperation is its own cross."

Isaac had assumed that he was going to have some dramatic effect on his friend's mood, but it was turning out to be just the opposite. He could scarcely believe what he was hearing from this man of the cloth.

"Evan, please. I understand that you have gone through a disconcerting period and that your life is in transition. But that is not reason enough, surely, to abandon your life's meaning? If you will just listen to what I have to say, and apply that wisdom of yours to helping me make some sense of it, perhaps we can both find some perspective."

The priest leaned back in his chair, barely able to contain his sarcasm.

"Fine, Isaac. You talk, I'll listen. Then I'll dispense of that sage advice I have handed out to my congregation over the years like Halloween candy...or a tasty placebo."

Isaac could only shake his head in frustrated confusion. They sat there with only the sound of the hissing logs between them. Two old men, consumed as they had always been with questions of faith and eternity.

Evan had kept his cancerous doubt inside of himself for too long. And in spite of Isaac's annoyance, he was going to get some things off his chest for a change...while there was yet time.

"You know, the Jesuits have a saying: 'To have sinned is good.' Meaning, of course, that there are valuable lessons to be learned after the fact of sin. Life, then, can be seen as a series of transgressions and penance that ultimately will lead the flawed and the faithful to salvation.

"But where does that leave someone like myself? What does that say about the men and the women who just seem to make a habit of doing the right thing? I will never be a St. Augustine because I didn't lead a life of debauchery and heresy before I 'saw the light.' I walked the same uninspired path all my life. There was no 'crisis of conversion' for me...no born-again awakening. It has all been so routine, like toiling away in some anonymous factory, stamping out the same, tired product...like a staple, or a bobby-pin...one of those necessary items that no one takes particular notice of. Then one day you're seventy-five years old. They shake your hand and send you on your way. On your way out the door, you look back over your shoulder and see that the conveyor belt is moving right along. Everything is running quite smoothly without you. You weren't vital at all. And you won't be missed in the slightest.

"I forgive people every Saturday afternoon as my own spirit has declined into a moral tar-pit. I have taken the long, circular path to the same point I have allegedly steered so many others from. Now it is I who am the wayward and the misguided. I am lost and empty, and there is no going back—for I have already been there. I have led, and cannot follow."

He walked to the bar and poured himself another healthy shot of Isaac's brandy. After swallowing several times and refilling, he turned back to Isaac with his new world-view.

"I may be a little late to the dance, but there are still a few ticks left on this grandfather clock. I'm going to finish this bottle of brandy because I have only been drunk once in my entire life—and spent a week in prayer trying to atone for it—and I'm going to offer a back rub to the next woman I meet. I don't even care if she's married. I'll even use the Lord's name in vain, if I should take the notion.

"I survived a World War. I watched as the world became uglier than it did beautiful, christened hundreds of babies and married hundreds of couples who no longer speak to one another. But somewhere along that fine line I toed so dutifully, I lost something vital of myself. I buried, and kept burying, the questioning, passionate Evan Connor for the sake of a calling that I may never have actually been called to. What voice did I think I heard when I was still a lonely, misunderstood, Irish teenager? Why did I think that this is where I should end my days?"

"Evan!"

Isaac elbowed his way rudely into the priest's monologue. It was time to bring Evan, kicking and screaming, into the present.

"I have met a vampire."

"...and I may be feeling sorry for myself, but for once I am going to...uh. What did you just say, Isaac?"

Isaac felt the blood drain from his extremities. There was a potent shock associated with the utterance of those words. As though some residual blood-marriage with Julian yet remained.

"I said that I have met a vampire. I also had dinner, drinks, and conversation with him."

"Well then. That's just fine, Isaac. I understand that the church is forming a spring bowling league. Perhaps you and your new friend could work on your handicaps."

"I am deadly serious about this, Evan. Now. Are you going to hear me out?"

Now he definitely had the priest's attention. Even the tumbler hung slack in his hand. He offered his first advice of the day.

"I want you to take a healthy swig of that stuff, count to twenty, and tell me once more that you are serious."

Isaac filled his glass and began with his walk in the park in Atlanta. Over the course of the next two hours he covered every detail, his voice alternating from matter-of-fact monotone to excited exuberance. The priest sat very still throughout, revealing nothing of his thoughts, moving only to refill his glass. But try as he might, he could no longer hope for inebriation.

Isaac finished his story with his vampire walking away through the unsuspecting populace of Jackson Square. He sighed deeply, like a man suddenly pronounced innocent on the steps of the guillotine.

Evan finally broke the lengthy silence that followed Isaac's story.

"We are both old, my friend, and may therefore be suspect in the matters of memory and the recall of details. We might well be forgiven for embellishment...a little garnish to spruce up the stale dish of our days. I will admit that, in all the years I have known and conversed with you, I have rarely seen more conviction. You speak the truth as you know it. I understand your hesitancy with this matter. And I sincerely appreciate your confidence in relating it to me now. But you must also appreciate my skepticism. The man that you describe is obviously insane. Convincing, perhaps. But most insane."

"That was precisely my own reaction to it all, Evan. But I can assure you that he is...perhaps it is now 'was'...not insane. However, if it will make it more palatable to you, we may speak of him hypothetically. Because I simply must have your opinions on some questions that are vexing me."

"If you will humor me...and let us assume that the man I met was, indeed, a vampire...if such a creature does exist, and if he has spent some six hundred years trying to become better than his nature dictates, despite tragedy after heartbreak after betrayal…then might this not imply a divine spark in ourselves that is worthy of our efforts to fan it into full flame? The man has suffered disproportionately. Yet he clings stubbornly to a faith in the salvation of love."

"This may be a little complicated, but try to follow me here." He smiled broadly to assure the priest that he wasn't usurping his omniscience. "Julian, the vampire, related to me many fantastic stories that rang of truth, but there was one in the cathedral in New Orleans that you might find of interest. It was an experience that convinced him we live in a love-driven universe. He had certainty that his individual soul was of the deepest value. And it became his greatest motivation to share that with me…the ultimate skeptic."

Isaac walked to the fireplace mantle and picked up the amber sphere, rolling it gently between his fingers. He debated sharing its secret with Evan, but something restrained him.

"If we assume that he was telling the truth—and I have many reasons to believe that he was—wouldn't his faith be a kind of indicator…a sort of proof of God's existence?"

Evan waved his hands in an expression of his annoyance.

"You still don't understand, do you, my friend? There is no 'proof.' You have wanted this from the beginning. When you first came to me so desperate and lost, and I thought that I could assure you. We were both so very naive. And we are just as naive now. Even a bona fide vampire would offer no proof, no matter how pious he might be. He would be no different than any mortal. Perhaps he would have experiences that he couldn't explain, which, when combined with his fervent desire for proof, he would be too eager to attribute to the hand of some grey-bearded being who sits around just waiting for our prayers to arrive so that he can leap into action on our behalf…and on behalf of the other seven billion souls down here wallowing in our own filth. His entire delusion could well be some deranged need to experience what he thinks is the 'eternal.' He kills, goes into denial, and then sees some divine intervention that forgives and reassures. Pretty common stuff for the psychopath, I'm afraid. Whatever he is, he has to struggle right along with the rest of us. As do you, my dear friend. I'm sorry. But there is nothing here to give you any more hope than anything else, Isaac."

Isaac was crestfallen. He had expected so much more than this out-of-hand dismissal.

"I can't believe that this is the same Evan Connor I have known and admired for most of my adult life. There was a time when you would have been the one admonishing me for my narrow-minded skepticism. You would have at least been intrigued. And whether or not you were convinced of the man's identity, you would have been curious about the details of his faith, and perhaps pursued it all for the sake of another lost soul's comfort. You are offering the sort of understanding that I offered the man myself…which was little.

"It is reflection that has shown me how I failed him. I have to believe that Julian is who he claimed to be. But he is also more than he claimed. And this is what has possessed me for the past several months. What was it that he wanted me to understand? Not believe…but *understand*."

"Alright, Isaac, take it easy. You have become too emotionally involved in this man's affairs. I suspect that, in telling him the details of your life with Lessa, you may have unearthed some rather persistent and potent ghosts."

"That may be true, Evan. But there is something I am missing here that I feel certain could bring me a better understanding of this eternity question. Time and again, Julian showed me a compassion I have rarely witnessed. In the process he summed up his entire history…a sort of putting affairs in order. It was crucial to him that I comprehend his motives, that I see it all from his perspective. In the end, he was so very certain of some benevolent hand behind all that had transpired."

"Maybe," Evan spoke softly, kindly, "what he needed was your forgiveness. You obviously harbored some vicarious hatred for the man, left over from the bitter dregs you swallowed under the Nazis. For him, your forgiveness may well have been as valuable as God's. I sense some truth in that."

"You are right, to a point. That is enough to show me that I have missed yet another opportunity to do something noble. Will my anger forever sentence me to coldness? The man was no Nazi. I knew this. But he was the best thing going on the hate parade. It was too easy to lay some of my loss at his doorstep. Damn."

"Well. It is done now, Isaac. The poor creature has moved on to another chapter of his life. You can learn something from that and do the same. And I think you should start with a call to the police. I still believe that what you have described is a deeply disturbed human being…a man. Not a monster. They might be able to find him and get him some help."

A mocking laugh broke from Isaac's throat.

"If he is a vampire, Evan, they will never find him. And if he isn't…well. They certainly won't be interested in helping him."

"Hmmm. I will leave that to your better judgment. But I will remind you of one thing. In spite of the ghastly scene in Birmingham, you never actually witnessed this man doing any of the morbid things that mythological vampires are supposed to do. The thing with the girl in the club, Erica, could easily have been staged. The simple transference of twenty dollars could accomplish the trick. Be wary, Isaac. You know as well as anyone that this species is capable of almost any horror. And it will go to as many lengths to justify them."

"As always, Evan, I respect your opinions. But you lack my experience with the man."

"Well, you sleep on it, Isaac. I have to be on my way. I am sorry that I wasn't more of a comfort to you. And I am sorry that I can't seem to take it all more seriously. Now, I will wish you a pleasant evening. I am feeling suddenly quite tired."

Isaac walked his friend to the door. As Evan passed into the chill, night air, Isaac had a sudden thought to call him back. But Evan walked on determinedly, and Isaac bolted the door behind him. He walked back to the fire, then settled heavily into his chair. He watched the last embers go singly out.

Chapter Eighteen

Evan Connor leaned back against the porcelain incline of his tub. He watched the steam vapors rise and curl above the surface of the water, then spiral lazily toward the ceiling. Everything was moist heat and careless intention. Everything but the cold, malevolent wafer of steel balanced between his thumb and forefinger.

He had read that this was the best way. The warm water would coax open the pores and the blood would flow freely, painlessly, with a minimum of mess for those who would come later. One only needed to pull the plug from the drain, and Evan Connor would flow into the sewers of the world.

It was an intriguing thought, this death…and how his life would swirl above the drain…the little whirlpool of what he had once been, now rushing among secret rusty places, mingling with the offal and waste of a thousand lives, a thousand dreary dreams…the flushing and the rinsing of filth and refuse. What he had once been…what he had once been. And now, what he was about to become.

Would they wrap the dangling ends of his exhausted body against the curious eyes of his neighbors, the strange men and women in various uniforms and badges that gave them privilege over his dignity? Would someone say, "Here, cover him with this. He was a priest, after all?"

Would there be whisperings and nods of silent understanding? Would someone offer that the cancer was too much for him to bear? Would anyone wonder that it might be something more than that? Would a pretty, young woman look at the wounds on his wrists and wonder at what longings might once have pulsed there?

The priest ran his hands along the length of his body. It was an odd sensation. For a moment, they lingered on his genitals. He had never known the physical ecstasies that so many other men had known with women. He never would. And he guessed, now, that it would not have mattered in the greater scheme of things if he had, just once, responded to one of those warm squeezings of the hands, or the suggestive hugs against full, lonely bosoms.

Would it have been so damned damnable if he had dared to indulge in that peculiar pleasure that God's own poets have written so eloquently of? Would it have cast him into the fiery pits, forever, without pardon? Or would it have been the crisis that, like St. Augustine, would have moved him to a deeper relationship with the divine?

It hardly seemed to matter now. He sighed deeply and watched the steam move upon his breath. Everyone had regrets. Everyone had need and motive, desire and impetus…and everyone, in the end, created their own morality. His best friend had, just tonight, shown him that.

It had pained him to listen to the sad, desperate pleas as they fell like prayers from Isaac's lips. Was God so far removed from Man that he was forced to create fantasies of angels and demons to fill in? It had been a pitiful display of the species' unfulfilled longing to know the elusive entity called "God." Vampires. A man who had survived the atrocity of all atrocities, only to come to a delusional dead-end where murderers create entire narratives devoid of salvation.

It was enough. Evan didn't need to see any more. He was seventy-eight years old and could offer proof of nothing. Nor, for that matter, a halfway-firm conviction. All he had learned had eventually been proven wrong. Now there was only the vaguest sort of sorrow associated with that realization. And even that, even sorrow, was something he had never experienced at the level so many others had.

Well. This death, waiting there just beyond the next whisper of the clock, was something that would be uniquely his. The orchestration of it, at any rate, would be his.

If there had been any doubt about robbing the cancer of its victory, it had been removed by Isaac's troubling dialogue. The razor blade that waited there like an indifferent servant would soon become his one and only act of defiant independence. This was his call, his decision. There was no more wondering at what God or the Church would want from him. Those things had mattered too much, for too long. They had mattered to Isaac, too. What good had it done either of them? His friend was senile and he, the decrepit priest, was faithless.

"Oh, God…why do you lead us, like cripples of hopelessness, to such despair? Do you require our abject surrender before you will save us?"

His head fell back upon the rim of the tub and he stared up at the ceiling with swollen, accusing eyes. The silence. Always, the only answer…that indifferent, apathetic silence. How, then, are these prayers supposed to retain any dynamic? How, then, are they to avoid the numbness of routine, of empty habit? If only one prayer were to be answered with anything else but that infinite silence…

Evan glanced briefly back upon the thread of his life. Was there anything that he could have done differently? Some alternative path that might not have led to this warm tub and this cold steel?

But that was foolish speculation. Everyone, every single mortal, was forced to choose and choose again, each day. The small, seemingly-insignificant choices carried as much weight and consequence as any others. If one were to look back at all the divergent roads, wouldn't half those roads be chosen differently now…if they could be? And the deeper question of all: would it have really mattered if they were?

There were regrets, of course. And a man alone with a razor can accuse himself with them all. There had even been a woman. One that mattered above all others. Typically, she had come into his life when a decision had already been made…when the seal had been pressed, and the envelope delivered. Funny he should think of her now.

If he had decided to stay with her, to renounce his decision for the priesthood, would he be any happier today? Would he be watching the play of light as it skipped and balanced like a mercury-life upon the mirror of the blade?

It did no good to ponder on such folly. It did no good to remember how her scent embraced him through the lattice of the confessional when she came into the quietly-shadowed country church where he had started, fresh from her walks along the cliffs above the Irish Sea. Or how she would try to catch her breath, while she whispered that she hadn't done anything really worth confessing…and oh, he knew that it was true. Just as he knew how he wished the two of them had done something very much worth confessing, together. Just as he also knew that he would have to walk seven miles to the next village after she had gone, to confess to his own desires to the young priest there.

It did no good to recall that one glorious afternoon, when he had been out in the intoxicating sea air himself, secretly hoping to cross paths with her, and she had come up over the hill, the wind snapping against the hem of her skirt, revealing those muscular calves and even a hint or two of her firm, round thighs. The sight of her against the sky and the sea had been like a poem…a sonnet of holy flesh and radiant spirit. They had fallen in stride together, with few words necessary between them, the sighs of the wind more than enough language to bind them to their heart's desire. A desire that led them to the privacy of a few stunted trees tucked into a windbreak of warm moor-stone and sunshine. A primordial intent that found her breath and her lips and her every cell encouraging her breasts into his trusted hands…and into his mouth. And her hands so summer-eager in his trousers, and the way he lay on his back and watched the clouds spiral into myriad forms before giving way to the formless. He knew a different kind of love in that moment, different than the love of an abstract savior. The idea leapt all bright and fully-painted in his mind that the only religion that mattered, the only one that was authentic in its potential, was the religion he had just that moment discovered as her hands and her lips danced exquisite circles on his body. That thought—that the love between two committed souls was the only religion that could truly save ANY one—suddenly turned from light to darkest, thunderous shadow…and terrified his mortal soul. He had pushed her away against her protests, shaming them both with his actions. They had gathered their things and fled from their Garden…forever.

It did no good to recall seeing her years later in London with her husband and child…and how it had seemed a betrayal. Not by her, but by life, or something like it. He wouldn't have felt that way at all if he had never had to see her again, if he could have kept his secret memories of her somehow sealed away from everything else. If he could have made them invulnerable to all disappointment. But she had been there, in London, when

Ireland was her home. When Ireland should have been, forever, their place.

He had felt strangely uneasy with prayer for a long while afterwards. In his mind, he had given God everything of himself. Was he now allowed to keep a memory, something separate from the sacrifice and hardship of his calling?

It did no good. He had followed the path that had led him here. Even though it had seemed to be one continuous path, he could see now that it had been many. It did no good to question, to wonder, to regret. The end was the inevitable thing. And he had reached his.

His faith had never really been tested. It had just been pressed into service for too long against the grinding-stone of his circumstances. As he brought the paper-thin sliver of steel into contact with his wrist, he understood that *that* had been the problem all along.

The blade lingered upon the blue thread showing through his pale skin. That was the path he needed to follow now. For once there was no mystery. The direction was clear. He needed only to trace the steel along that blue ribbon of life, and it would take him where he wished to go…someplace new and uncharted. Someplace different than this.

He pressed the blade into his skin and watched the first reaction of blood as it rose like an eager bride to its marriage with the steel. But suddenly he stopped. There was one thing left to do. It would be a mortal sin not to call Isaac and say goodbye.

He must be careful not to arouse Isaac's suspicions. But he was obligated to give his friend something to look back upon after he was gone. Something that Isaac would later be able to identify as a farewell. There was too much between them for Evan to selfishly remove himself without any acknowledgment of that fact.

He rose from the tub and wrapped a washcloth around his bleeding wrist, then wrapped a robe around his body. He composed a few lines in his head as he made his way to the phone.

"Hello, Isaac. I just wanted to call and let you know that I have appreciated your friendship over the years..."

No, that definitely would get Isaac's alarms going.

"Hey, Isaac. I wanted to tell you how much I enjoyed our conversation tonight. It's been my great pleasure to have been your confidante and friend..."

That was still too close. To Hell with the script, he could make it up as he went along. The important thing was just to call him so that he would know later that he had been thought of.

But Isaac wasn't answering. Neither was his machine. And, according to their old plan, that was definitely something to be concerned about.

All thoughts of suicide vanished as Evan raced around his bedroom for his clothes and shoes. Why hadn't Isaac engaged his machine if he was going out? Evan knew that he wouldn't overlook that. He took a deep breath and willed himself to calm down. It wasn't that big a deal, really. But it was. Especially in light of what Isaac had shared with him just a few hours before.

Their system had been in place for some fifteen years. And Isaac had never forgotten. Evan dressed quickly and headed off in the direction of Isaac's home.

Chapter Nineteen

With his company gone and no work to distract him, Isaac had gone out for some exercise with the neighborhood cats. The full moon made him feel like a lost hunter, alone among the silhouetted ruins of some ancient jungle city. The big, carnivorous cats were everywhere, lurking just beyond the shadows, darting forth with hisses and growls intended to unnerve him.

For most of an hour, he had chased after them with his raised broom. It rested now in the corner of his study like a faithful ally. He had thrown a couple of sturdy logs on the fire and it was blazing anew as he read from *Black Elk Speaks*.

The circle of light from his chair-side lamp was, aside from the fire, the only brightness in the house. Beyond that circle were shadowed books and dusty furniture. And the watchful eyes of Julian Germain.

Julian had been standing in the shadows for some time. At the moment, his eyes were locked upon the "key" that had given him access to Julian's home. A key that Julian had intentionally placed into Isaac's care. A personal and cherished piece of property that allowed the vampire access. In this case, the locket bearing the ashes of Joan of Arc.

While it was true that vampires could only enter private domiciles by invitation, they could pass unobstructed across the threshold of any building where the energies of a "public" were welcome. The only way around the invitation into a private dwelling was to have something of personal worth to a vampire already inside. Julian had anticipated this day. While the gift was a genuine offering, he knew it would come in handy in short order. And so it had.

He was enjoying Isaac's choice of music. It was Chopin, and it lulled Isaac into slumber. He watched the old man dozing and felt a pang of sympathy. How many nights had he settled beside that fire, alone, dreaming of his Lessa?

Julian had come to finish their business. Enough time had passed for Isaac to have considered all the details and possible meanings of their acquaintance. He should be ripe for the final drama.

Julian stepped forward into the circle of light and cleared his throat. Isaac jerked his head up from his chest and caught his breath.

"Julian?!?"

"Hello again, Isaac. It's so good to see you."

The next several minutes passed with Isaac searching among the turbulent vortex of his thoughts for his voice and his composure. Julian moved calmly about the study reading the titles of Isaac's books, and peering at the photographs on the mantle. He gave the startled old man all the time he needed to consider the implications of Julian's return. He took a picture of Lessa from the mantle. She was in the middle of a group of young people, smiling. It was then that Isaac broke his reverie.

"Somehow, I knew that I would see you again. But I didn't expect it to be here, in my home. Why have you come here?"

Julian returned the picture to the shelf.

"Because the incomplete feelings that you have known, I have known as well."

He sighed deeply and lowered himself onto the divan.

"I assure you that this will, indeed, be our final meeting. I have come to ask you a favor. Now that you have had these past months to consider all that has transpired, I believe you will be in the frame of mind to oblige me. Especially when you have heard the things that I am going to reveal to you."

Isaac felt an involuntary shiver dance along the notches of his spine as a stone of tension settled upon his stomach. He well knew that he needed to hear all the vampire had to say. And how dearly he dreaded it.

Julian could see the unease drawing at the corners of Isaac's mouth.

"Some of what I have to tell you will not be easy for you to hear. But, after I have gone, I am certain you will know the same peace I hope to find for myself. Our fates have become…no. Our fates have long been…entwined, Isaac."

The vampire reached into the folds of his overcoat and produced a plain manila envelope. He laid it carefully on the table between them. Isaac's universe suddenly seemed to shift orbits, revolving end over end around that envelope.

"When I have gone," Julian spoke deliberately, "I want you to read the single piece of paper you will find enclosed there. To say that it is a gift from eternity would be an understatement. I am merely the messenger. But the message is one that saved me. And I am most certain it will do the same for you.

"But before you are granted this gift, you will be asked to perform the favor I mentioned. If you refuse this favor, that envelope will remain in my care until you change your mind. The favor is this. You must take my life."

Isaac felt the air rush from his lungs.

"Dear God, Julian! I can't possibly oblige you! And you can't possibly be serious!"

Julian spoke calmly, as though detached from the very words he uttered.

"Listen to me carefully now, Isaac. When I have told you what I am here to tell you, you too will see the inevitability in all this. The situation may seem distasteful, but it is the perfect summary to everything we have journeyed toward. This is not my decision, or even yours. The contents of that envelope are proof that this has all been a working process…that there has been a plan to all of it…and that our faith is never wasted. I say again, this is our passage to true and lasting peace. But there is some work yet to be done before we can rest."

Julian rose and began to pace. Isaac knew him well enough by now to know that he paced when he had the full measure of ideas and dreams to consider.

"Here is the summation of the story—our story—as I know it. You will recall that, throughout my six-hundred-year history, I have preyed primarily on the disadvantaged and dying. If you look at the parallel history of mankind, you will see clearly that I have had ample opportunity to sate my hunger. What I mean is, there have been times and places where I could linger for months and years at a time, and the machines of human slaughter would keep me fed. It was almost enough that I could survive as more a scavenger than a predator, really.

"Wherever there was widespread death and destruction, I and those like me could be found…like stray dogs around a landfill. The plagues of Europe. The famines of Africa. Let's not even talk of the incessant wars that your kind find so enthralling. And how we came to the Second World War…the SECOND one. As though the first one shouldn't have been more than enough to convince us of our own psychosis. No, the second one produced even more unbridled, lustful carnage than the bloody first. It served up to those like me the fattest part of history's hog…the Holocaust."

Now Isaac rose from his chair and he, too, began to pace. The two of them moved around the room like tragic characters performing the final act of some Greek tragedy.

"It was all too easy, too convenient not to take advantage of. My work was all but done for me. I needed only to step in at the last moment, just before the final breath was drawn, and feed at my leisure. Other than avoiding the daylight, and the unlikely curiosity of the rest of the walking dead, there was no fear of reprisal... no one was going to conduct an autopsy of the bloodless victims already emaciated and dying. As a predator, my conscience was quite clear. None of this gruesome disposal of sentient beings was my doing. This horror fell squarely on the shoulders of the HUMAN beings. For once, I could feed without the slightest twinge of guilt."

"You know the score, Isaac. Dozens of your people perished each night from starvation, disease, suicide, or sheer loss of will. This isn't even considering the gas chambers or the point-blank bullets behind the ear. I would simply enter the camps each night, choose the weakest of all the weak ones, and end the nightmare of those places for him or her forever. Who knows, Isaac, you and I may have passed in the night long before that dark park in Atlanta drew our paths together again."

Isaac was standing in the corner of the room, his face concealed in the shadows. But Julian could guess at the painful distortions wearing at and eroding his features, like the flood of Noah moving over the landscape of his heart.

"Stop trembling, Isaac. And listen to what miracles are possible in this tired drama you know as life...

"In the terrible winter of 1944 and '45, my feeding ground was the largest and most despicable of the death camps...the camp you knew as intimately as I did. Auschwitz. Near the end of that camp's existence, in the days before it was liberated by the Russian Army, a strange and portentous thing occurred.

"It was about ten p.m. I was in the woods bordering the village of Birkenau. Isaac...please, gather yourself. I came upon the bodies of five men and three women...it's all right. Patience, my friend. Bear with me for just a while longer. The eight of them had been shot sometime during the day…"

Isaac was sobbing openly now. Julian could see his shoulders quaking from across the room.

"Steady now, Isaac. One of the women was still alive…but barely. She was unable to speak and she had lost a great deal of blood. I knew that she would perish very soon. Normally, I would have considered feeding on her to hasten the end to her suffering. But I knew, I sensed, that this was a different encounter.

"I held her in my arms. Her long, dark hair fell across my lap where her head lay. She looked into my eyes with a warmth and tenderness that I have never forgotten. There was an understanding there…"

Now Julian's voice broke as well, despite his willing against it. That was more than Isaac could bear. He threw himself back into his chair and covered his ears.

"That picture there, on the mantle, does your wife no justice. Next to my Clara, Lessa was the single most noble creature I have ever encountered. I am eternally grateful that I was able to give her some final contact that was not brutal, that was not evil. Not evil, Isaac. Do you understand me? That last look in Lessa's eyes was one of peace…and gratitude."

Julian pulled a handkerchief from his pocket and wiped at his eyes, then offered it to Isaac.

"Before she died, she took my hand and placed it over the breast pocket of her shirt. I reached into that pocket and pulled out a folded piece of paper. Without that piece of paper I would never have known you, all these years later, for who you are. And this situation we have found ourselves in the midst of would have been just another in a long line of bizarre circumstances for me. As it stands, that piece of paper, and all that has happened since that day, is proof enough for me that your wife awaits you…and that the eternal love you and I have spent our lives in search of is no longer a thing to be doubted or guessed at."

Just then the phone began to ring, and ring incessantly. Isaac rose and turned on the overhead light in the room. But Julian grabbed his wrist before he could get to the receiver. Isaac spun and looked into Julian's face, stunned by how much the vampire had aged during the past few months. Something vital had gone from his demeanor. There was only resignation to a less than joyous fate. He was ready to die.

"This is why you must take my life, Isaac. Do you understand? Here is your salvation from hatred, from anger, right here in this envelope. And here is my only chance for a peace of my own. I cannot fall on the stake myself. I won't ignore the events that have transpired in the past months. You and I were brought together precisely for this night. Now, accept your responsibility."

Isaac rushed to the bar and uncorked his best bottle of Cognac, then drank straight from the bottle. Julian stood calmly in the background, waiting patiently for Isaac to accept the inevitable.

Isaac drank and paced, paced and drank. He knew that if he didn't follow through, if he didn't grant the vampire his macabre request, he would never read the contents of that envelope. But the thought of impaling Julian on a stake horrified and repulsed him. He just couldn't imagine it. But he knew that he must. And that, somehow, he would.

The sudden knock at the door startled them both. Julian motioned for Isaac to stand still. He began moving toward the door when a key was inserted and the door flew open, revealing the flushed and eager face of Father Evan Connor.

Evan looked around the room quickly, surveying the scene for signs of a struggle. Satisfied at least temporarily of his friend's safety, he made his way to the bar.

"Damn it, Isaac! I thought we agreed that you would engage that blasted answering machine. You didn't answer your phone.

Your machine didn't answer your phone. So naturally I came scrambling over here like a fool. Would you care to tell me exactly what is going on?"

Isaac was muted by the sudden turn of events. Julian filled in the blanks.

"I'm afraid that Isaac is in a mild state of shock. Please. Allow me to introduce myself. I am Julian Germain."

The freshly-filled glass fell from Connor's hand, tumbled gracefully, and proceeded to spray its contents around the room like a ruptured jugular.

"A waste of good brandy, Father," Julian observed dryly.

"The vampire wants me to take his life, Evan."

Isaac had regained his voice, but his words only added to the surrealism seeping into the priest's world in place of alcohol. Evan looked around the room, found the familiar comfort of his favorite chair, and sank into it to stare at a piece of shadow on the far wall.

Julian walked back to the bookcase. He stood before it for several, silent minutes, then withdrew a volume of Blake's poetry, turned some pages, and read aloud.

"I have traveled through a Land of Men,
A Land of Men and Women too,
And heard and saw such dreadful things
As cold Earth wanderers never knew."

He replaced the book and turned to face the stunned, and all too weary, old men.

"And now, Isaac, I will finish the fourth act. As I read the words on that piece of paper I pulled from Lessa's shirt…"

Evan shot from his chair, startled back to reality by Julian's words.

"What nonsense is this? What is he saying? He mentions your wife's name so casually and you sit there as though he was discussing the weather! What bold madness is this?"

Isaac started to speak but Julian waved his reply aside with one of his own.

"I am afraid that I cannot tolerate any interruptions from you, Reverend. Your timing is most unfortunate. I am no longer surprised by the shifting circumstances of this matter. But the hour is already late, and this must be concluded tonight. Now, you will sit quietly and absorb what you can or I will be forced to restrain you in one of the other rooms. It is your choice."

Evan hesitated for just a moment, then started for the door, speaking over his shoulder as he walked.

"I will not be a party to this lunacy! I am concerned for your safety, Isaac. As *you* should be. I am going for the police."

The vampire reached the door ahead of the ailing priest. He stood there calmly, waiting for Evan's next move. Evan stopped in his tracks, considering. He didn't have to ponder for long, as Julian's next monologue assured them all of the priest's participation.

"In the early days of the Church's mission, the priests and clerics would wander the known world at their own peril. This required great courage and commitment to their cause. Or maybe it just required a blind loyalty to some fantasy of a well-reward afterlife. Either way, they managed to learn a few survival techniques as they went along. If they became ill, for example, there was nothing for them but whatever they could gather from the fields and the hedgerows in which they found themselves. Things have changed dramatically since then. You must have an excellent healthcare plan. Is that not so, Father?"

"What on earth are you going on about, man?" Evan shot a desperate glance at Isaac, who could only shrug his shoulders. This was strictly Julian's show.

"What I am 'going on about,' good Padre, is the fact that we are tending to the business of eternal life here this evening. But you have brought the stink of death upon us. You come here out of some secondary concern, some habitual regard for an old friend, yet it is I who am trying to steer him toward the divine. What place do you have here? The rot consuming you is more than just a cancer. Despite that, I suspect that you too have some role to play. Yes. In fact, it may just be that you *need* to be here, as we do. That fresh wound on your wrist is proof enough, I imagine. Now return to your seat, Father, while I attempt to pry open that mind you are trying so hard to seal away from the miracles of the world."

Evan was floored. This man knew he was dying. He looked again at Isaac, who walked over and placed a hand upon his shoulder.

"Why haven't you told me, Evan? How long have you known this?"

Julian interrupted them again.

"There is no time now. You will have to deal with these revelations later, gentlemen."

He ushered them back to their seats, refilled their glasses like an attentive host, and resumed.

"As I was saying. While reading those words…it was as though I were hearing a voice come to me from some far place, as one hears sounds traveling great distances over still waters. It was the voice of my dear, lost Clara reading the words from the page. I knew then that she really was waiting, just as your Lessa waits for you. So. Once again, we return to that envelope and its sacred contents. But you will never gaze upon them if you refuse me this regrettable, but necessary, request."

The three of them stared blankly at one another, each waiting for the others to act.

"Evan," Isaac spoke softly. "You have to help me with this. I cannot do it alone."

"I will be damned first!"

Evan leaped from his chair and stalked the room like a caged lion. Julian had a sudden epiphany. His words froze the priest like a January pond.

“Father, I am Catholic. I request your prayers and the sacrament of the Last Rites.”

The priest whirled, stuttering a choked reply.

“That’s impossible! You’re…you…”

“I was baptized some six hundred years ago.”

He watched Evan’s eyes widen to the size of watery moons, then…

“Forgive me, Father, for I have sinned. It has been several centuries since my last confession.”

Evan staggered towards him, grabbed his arm, and led him off to an adjoining room, slamming the door behind them.

Isaac walked numbly back to the bar, poured preposterously, and eyed the envelope that lay just six feet away. What was the proof that would finally give him peace? He started for the envelope, stopped, and returned to the bar. It was time to finally exercise some of the faith that had directed this entire drama. It was time to take things in their season.

After half an hour had passed, Isaac realized that the two men might be absent for some time. He moved back to the couch and stretched out. He pondered the contents of Julian’s envelope and a wan little smile teased the corners of his mouth. He allowed himself to appreciate the long-lost joy of it…a simple and heartfelt smile. In ten minutes he was fast asleep.

He woke to the gentle prodding of his old friend’s hand.

“Wake up, Isaac. It is very, very late and we have work to do. I believe we have the will of God to attend to.”

He rose and looked at the clock on the mantle. Three hours had passed. Julian stood in the doorway, composed as always. Isaac looked at Evan for some explanation.

"It is too fantastic. But I have no further doubts. There is a credibility that one cannot manufacture from reading history or listening to ancient tales at a grandfather's knee. The authentic wisdom of experience shines forth like a beacon of honest expression. This man has lived what he claims he has. His suffering is not a thing of fabrication. It cannot be argued with. Now, having said all that, I have not a clue as to how we should proceed."

Both men turned their attention to the vampire. Julian shrugged with feigned indifference and walked to the opposite corner, where Isaac's cat broom stood like a ready sentry. He picked it up and snapped it over his thigh, creating a jagged weapon. He handed it to Isaac, who was trembling noticeably.

"Isaac, you asked me some time ago if I had any dreams left. I have one that is similar to your own: you are aware of it. But I have another. It would never be a dream for mortal humans, who have learned to take the sun for granted. I dream of the way the new morning changes from dark shades to the subtle colors of light...then becomes the full expression of the day.

"After all this has been done, you will be full of posthumous gratitude for what I have given you. But I need your compassionate best intentions now, not later. Please," he whispered. "Don't give me time to reconsider."

"Wait!" Father Connor rushed suddenly from the room and into the kitchen. He returned after several minutes with a bottle of Chambertin and a loaf of bread. He cleared the envelope and other debris from Isaac's table, arranged the bread and the wine, and offered the communal prayer. Then he summoned Julian for his final Communion.

"The body and blood of Christ."

Julian wiped abrupt tears from his eyes. He thanked the priest without words and returned to where Isaac stood, waiting with a somber expression. The two men embraced.

Julian stood back, took the jagged end of the stake and placed it over his heart before whispering his last words.

"You send me to my rest and to my peace. You send me to my love."

Isaac set his jaw and whispered a prayer of his own. Then, with closed eyes, he leaned forward, pushing his weight against the paper-light essence of Julian's withered frame. He heard a small sigh, pressed harder still, then fell forward onto the floor. Julian was gone.

Evan rushed to help him to his feet. The two men stared into the empty place that Julian had occupied just moments before. The universe rolled around them. Nothing would ever seem ordinary again.

"He seemed to suffer very little…" Evan announced in a reverent awe. "Then he was gone. Just…gone…"

Evan poured another drink for them, and they stood before the picture window, staring out at the fading night, both too numb to speak. Gradually, the night gave way to the reassuring sun and the sapphire darkness surrendered to the pearl-blue genesis of the new day. To Isaac, it was the first new day in more than fifty years. The past had been fractured and cast away. He raised his glass to the liberated vampire and took a long, appreciative taste of his own difference.

Suddenly, he remembered that there was more. He bolted back to the table and found the envelope lying beside it on the floor. He grabbed it with fumbling hands that seemed foreign and uncertain. Unable to complete the simple task, he handed it to Evan, who opened it carefully at the sealed edges then handed the piece of paper to his abruptly-sober friend. Isaac sat down and began to read Lessa's last poem.

In middle day the dark storm came.
It caught us in the field where lovers lay.
We smelled it behind the trees,

You rose to leave, but
"Stay," I breathed.
Wind took the word,
But you had heard
And fell
With the first kiss of sky
To catch my hair. I sighed,
"Eden was never tame."
You cried, "We lost
This with the Garden."
I tried to feel the same,
But rain, and rain, was falling
To wash it green again.
The tempest raged
And called our names
"Come home!" for we
Have loved this way
Eternally.

He read the poem a dozen times, and then a dozen times more, his heart bursting like Chinese rockets with every line. Each time he read it, he was overwhelmed with a deeper and newer meaning. The tears flowing from his eyes threatened to stain the precious words, so he reluctantly handed it to Evan Connor. After a long while, he handed it back to Isaac, muttering simply, "My God."

Isaac had no words to express the power, and the confidence of that power, rushing over him, wave upon wave…Fear? Anger? What were they now? What had they ever really been? Lessa had always known it. It had taken a long time, but her final lesson had persisted and found him right there at home, in his own heart… the home she had never vacated.

He moved toward the kitchen, patting Evan on the shoulder.

"I'll make some coffee, Evan. And you can tell me about this secret you've been carrying. Then we'll discuss how we're going to beat it. After that, I'll tell you about Joan of Arc.

Chapter Twenty

Isaac's eyes fluttered open. Slowly, at first…oh-so-slowly. Shafts of sunlight extended like golden columns from the tops of the shutters down to the old, wood floors. The only movement, so subtle as to defy gravity, were the dust particles that hovered there in the sunbeams, before falling softly…softer than snow… to the floor.

It was Sunday morning. Isaac stretched his arms over his head, turned back the bed covers, and placed his feet on the warm planks of the sun-washed floor. Sunday. Spring-time. He could hear the birds in the eves outside his bedroom window.

He dressed in grey wool trousers, a white shirt, and a blue paisley tie, over which he buttoned a black Scottish cardigan. He grabbed a hat at the door. Stepping out into the morning light, the cobalt sky seemed like a freshly starched shirt adorned by the bright boutineer of the sun. He walked toward the distant spires, his steps light, lively. Life, in all its facets, called out from the leaf-glad trees and the swing-set-joys of the corner park. He was on his way to church, to see an old friend once more.

Along the way he paused to converse with neighbors, some of them moving in his direction. But mostly he indulged his thoughts…his vibrant imagination…and the possibilities of life.

Isaac could not conjure even the vaguest memories of his once-heavy heart.

So much darkness, and so many shadows. He had had to navigate them all. But there had always been a beacon of light there for him. Death camps and ghettos, what power had they held, after all? All that former fear, his pent-up hatred, even the foul self-loathing, had vanished like the mortal husk of Julian's weary frame. And what moved into their place was what Evan had often spoke of. That deep and abiding love. That liberation that had eluded him almost to the end.

All the characters in his life-drama had fulfilled their roles. In retrospect, their roles had been perfect and necessary...and all played out with impeccable timing. They had all been "right." Patrik, his courage and disapproving but enduring loyalty. Evan, his steadfast friendship, his mentoring...the very essence of the confidant and the tireless ally. Julian, and his deeply important lessons on how the longevity of grief may well be the proof-positive that love is, truly, eternal. Ageless, timeless, history in the moment...Julian. The eternal guardian of the sacred flame. Willing to carry the burden of grief for centuries if it meant even the possibility of holding his Clara again.

But more "right" than all of them had been Lessa. Her faith was hardly a faith at all. It was a certainty. While all the rest of them, including most of all himself, had struggled with faith on an *intellectual* level—and always against the backdrop of personal loss and tragedy—Lessa had *known* that love is above and beyond the darkest deeds of man's malformed heart. To her, it had been like sitting in a darkened theater, watching the images of the film flicker and move, shadows and light, the roles of the characters... and the tensions of the good guy versus the bad guy, the betrayals, the violence, and the melodrama...all of it seemed so real up there, spread out across the canvas of the big screen, that it could drag you in so deeply you might laugh in parts and shed genuine tears in others. But finally the lights come up, and you stretch your legs and walk right back out into the sunlight, the terrors and the intrigues of the film already a fading memory. What you had experienced wasn't any more real than your imagination.

Only a handful of people in the history of the world had been able to live life from that liberating perspective. Just before the Buddha became enlightened while sitting in the forest, his senses were assailed by the demons of lust and violence. Much like Jesus, who would have similar experiences in the desert five hundred years later, he was offered the world, and then threatened with torturous death if he refused it. In the midst of the onslaught, he reached his hand down to touch the Earth. "This alone is real," he said. And the incessant drama of the mind was defeated, forever. In essence, the Buddha got up and left the theater. This was the wisdom that they had all come to see before the final curtain came down. He was eternally grateful for the lesson.

He had arrived at the church. There were many, many people present…all come to show love and gratitude that had *also* once been in doubt. But no longer. He removed his hat, anointed and crossed himself, and entered the hall.

The old man stood at the rear of a long, solemn line. Up ahead, over the shoulders and bowed heads of the faithful, he could see the muted, mahogany resting place of his dear, devoted friend, Evan Connor. He took one step forward, and paused. One step forward, closer to salvation.

The End